ALSO BY MICHAEL FROST BECKNER

HITLER'S LOKI
Berlin Mesa

SPY GAME
The Aiken Trilogy
Muir's Gambit
Bishop's Endgame
Aiken in Check

KALEIDOSCOPE:
A SPY GAME SERIAL
4th of July
Birthday

A NATION DIVIDED
Volume I: Episodes 101-104
Volume II: Episodes 105-108
Volume III: Episodes 109-112

Praise for Michael Frost Beckner
&
SPY GAME

"Pass the popcorn!"
—*Amazon Editors' Pick*, Vanessa Cronin, Sr. Editor

"Brilliantly executed...First-class spy novels with a smart, gritty atmosphere."
—Charles Cumming, *New York Times & Sunday Times Best-selling Author of KENNEDY 35 and BOX 88*

"A thinking man's thriller... A real adrenaline blast... I loved it!"
—Robert Redford

—"There's nobody quite like Beckner. Cerebral and unvarnished...with dialogue so sharp it's like dancing on hot coals. You'll swallow this book whole." - I.S. Berry, *Author of THE PEACOCK AND THE SPARROW, A New Yorker & NPR Best Book of the Year*

"Michael Frost Beckner serves up a judicious blend of showy action, political intrigue, ticking-clock suspense, and CIA one-upmanship for mainstream entertainment."
—*Variety*

"There is nothing like *The Aiken Trilogy*... Laced with absurdity & stylistically daring ... Beckner [is] a razzle-dazzle showman at the top of the thriller heap."
—Editor's Pick, *Publishers Weekly*

"Beckner is one of the most unabashedly duplicitous writers I've ever encountered ... Brilliant work."
—Stephen England, *Best-selling Author of the SHADOW WARRIOR Series*

"Michael Frost Beckner is the rarest of spy novelists, a beautiful and compelling writer who also has a mastery of tradecraft and a deep understanding of how espionage really works."
—Joe Weisberg, *former CIA Officer and EMMY Award-winning creator of The Americans*

Kaleidoscope

A Spy Game Serial

Part 2:

Birthday

Michael Frost Beckner

MONTROSE STATION PRESS

Las Vegas
2024

Published in the United States Montrose Station Press LLC

LIBRARY OF CONGRESS CONTROL NUMBER: 2024910325

ISBN 9798990351738 (paperback)
ISBN 9798990351721 (ebook)

Printed in the United States of America

Jacket Design & Illustrations by Andrew Frost Beckner

FIRST EDITION 2024

For Joel

KALEIDOSCOPE:

BIRTHDAY

"'There are some things,' said the magician, 'which I have to tell you, whether you believe them or not. The trouble is, I can't help feeling there is one thing which I have forgotten to tell. Remind me to warn you about Guenever another time.'"

—T. H. White, *The Once and Future King*

Prologue

*T**HEY KILLED HIM?*

Rush of movement. Clatter of wheels. Rush of figures.

Clatter of steel. Black/yellow knight. Blue/red knight.

Voice fugue. Polyphonic. Contrapuntal. Harmonious. "Homicidal cut-throat injury... Female patient. Thirty-six years of age...encountered bleeding profusely...extremely restless...poorly responsive to commands..."

Steel hooves. Armored horses. Clatter.

Clatter of light crashing bright waves above. Rods of light. Direct corneal blasts.

Lids taped. Mouth taped.

Blue Knight gored. They killed him!

Sound swirl. Light swirl. Mind swirl.

Killed Michael?

Oscillating pink-orange light penetrating taped-shut eyelids. Figures swirl.

A lance through the blue knight's breastplate. Armored body bouncing dead across his horse's silk-draped rump.

Michael laughs. "Knights aren't real anymore!"

"Hypovolemic shock..."

—California/TV/surfer hair falling back from the sides of his boyish face. "He's not hurt, Linny. They're pretend. The horses are pretend. Ly-yyyynnnn, don't cry over pretend!"

"...breathing spontaneously, airway unobstructed...wound temporarily sealed to reduce blood loss..."

Round and round the merry-go-round. I'm okay/I'll be okay.

(Knights-are-pretend. The jousting-knights are pretend. This will make you feel better. You pick. The wooden painted horses. Wooden painted dragons wooden bear painted unicorn swan: up-and-down round-and-round "Turkey in the Straw"—I know that song.)

"BP: eighty over sixty; heart rate: one-fifty BPM."

"Respiratory: twenty-six BPM; SP-O-two sixty-eight percent..."

See the balloon man. Watching us.

"...horizontal cut-throat wound fourteen centimeters by four centimeters in size, extending from the posterior border of the sternocleidomastoid muscle—"

"Suction—"

Watches me crying watches Mommy push me to the merry-go-round he watches Michael.

"—to the opposite side sternocleidomastoid muscle. Thyroid and cricoid cartilage fractured, vocal cord exposure; one-millimeter laceration, superior right fold, second two-millimeter laceration inferior left fold—"

"They're all pretend horses, Linny, see?"

I see the balloon man.

"Suction..."

"Initiating laryngoscopic intubation. Suction..."

A balloon, Michael?

"Watch that rack!"

A red balloon of blood blows out the front of Michael's head.

"Getting profuse bleeding into the oropharynx. Suction. Found the leak. Intubate."

(Pretend Michael?)

"Introducing oxygen. Ten-L per minute... We have spontaneous bag movement."

Pretend Michael.

"Bilateral air entry and oxygen saturation: one hundred percent."

Oh, God—he wore Michael's stuff—Michael sent him/set him up to die?

A merry-go-round baggage carousel. A carousel to stop me crying.

"Vitals?"

Bloody, dead, ring, jacket—Not-Michael/pretend-Michael better than real Michael and a balloon man for Michael. For Mommy.

"BP: one hundred over seventy; heart rate: one-fifteen BPM. Respiratory: twenty-six BPM..."

"Surgical table ready."

All the knights are pretend.

"Wheels locked."

"Roller board positioned."

"Lifting patient."

"I want three of you: head, neck, shoulders."

Off the merry-go-round. I'm three. In my stroller (I want to walk Mommy says no). Michael is eight. And the balloon man right there. Hands Michael a Soviet red balloon.

"Transfer on one... Three. Two. One—"

(Why does he kiss Mommy?)

"Transferring."

Mommy happy. (Where's Daddy?) The balloon man is always there.

Touch of rubbered fingers, silver flashes, face shadows.

My fucking eyes taped-fucking-shut!

Soft, dabbing—must-be-cotton—inside my neck.

Oh-god-my-neck's-wide-open!

Too many people. Too many hands. All over me.

Blasting light.

Don't panic. Don't panic. Don't panic.

"Prepare ketamine, seventy-five milligrams..."

Michael happy. Recognized Kalay...kalay...

"Midazolam, one milligram..."

Floating away. I'm a balloon. Don't be sad, Lynn, you're only dying/not-dying/dying?

"Fentanyl one hundred micrograms..."

Doris. Fire. Hangman rope. How could you ask me such a terrible thing? (I told Silas yes.)

"Proceeding with tracheostomy."

Lynn's mind emptied. Memories. Guilt. Pain. Fell into a soothing blackness. Pulsated in rhythm to her smoothing breath, her stabilizing life.

♕ ♕ ♕

THE YEAR IS 1693. It is April 27th. A Monday morning, shortly after ten. Stubborn mist clings to the river's shore. A sedge fly hatch dusts and dances the water's surface. Fifty feet out, two cypress piles are driven into the bed of the Patuxent River by tobacco traders, Judah and Silvanus "Silas" Kingston. Abob on a heavy flatbed, they share their labors with a band of Piscataway tribesmen. Six warriors the Kingston brothers ransomed in the fall from the Iroquois, now indentured to the brothers' service. A term equal to half the period of their enslavement as allowed by English and Indian law.

The anchoring of the dock posts is witnessed by both the English Governor Copley and the Emperor of Piscataway—last of the tribal chieftains to join the League of Amity with the Maryland colony. This treaty allows the Piscataway chieftain individual authority to cede tribal lands of the Patuxent People to private colonial ownership; to draw personal profit from commerce made by this cession.

The sinking of these piles marks the birth of Foxtail Farm. A child born in sin; born of a marriage of convenience between two disparate societies for mutual profit.

An icehouse for animal carcasses, for pelts, constructed next. Followed by the original manor house—known to the current Kingston Family as the North Vista Outhouse—back of the tobacco fields on the bluffs above.

A wharf and the permanent dock that extends another fifty feet from the original posts—red maple planks; capable of servicing ocean-going vessels—completed in 1697. Soon vibrant with the shouts of robust men, the hammer crack and wubwub rasp of saws and the smack of lumber; the clunk of blocks/creak of rope/clang of brass; the cacophony of gulls above the slap of fish spilled from nets. Bells, always bells. And whistles. And the constant groan of the wood beneath, in unending conversation with the rolling water. All this, timed to take full advantage of the 1698 law that legalizes the trafficking of human chattel from Africa.

A wharf house/trading post/customs shed managed by Turkey John Swann. A loving husband, fair boss, kind father; the only one of the Piscataway Indians who remains in the employ of the brothers Kingston at the culmination of his servitude. In the Maryland colony, he will become the most famous and fearsome tracker/scalphunter of runaway slaves. No man, woman, or child ever escaped the tomahawk, whip, and rope of Turkey John Swann. But it is the tobacco leaf that brings the gold. Provides for the second manor constructed on the bluff top where the ninety-eight acres of Foxtail Farm loom. A plantation high and mighty, heaped in wealth and vested in damnation.

Nights fill with music and candlelight. Food and wine and song and dance. Romance. Foxtail Farm is the center of light and enlightenment, where, for a time, the entire colony fluxes glittering.

But of all this river activity—labor, commerce, humanity (and its opposite), delight (and despair)—all that endures are the two cypress piles.

Weakened by time.

Weakened by current.

Wreaked by storms too many to count.

Left to decay by indolent neglect. Only their broken heads remain. Jagged, splintered tops. Sides smoothed by the ebb and flow of tides. Sides smoothed and cascaded by dark Patuxent River grass. Fluffed and bright with pickle green algae.

*"Our green mermaids. Always watching over us."
Lynn to her brothers, her mother, and—if he ever listened—her father, those playful, splashing, swimming
summers on the strip of sandy shore at the bottom of this
family's ramshackle wooden stairs. Two cypress piles
bobbing into sight and out with the play of wind above.
The current below speaks to the mermaids.*

*To Doris, they've moved her—always—as the heads
of children. Sacrificed. Drowned. She's never said so because, were she asked why, Doris would reveal a darker
nightmare. A shipwreck entirely of babies strewn along
the river bottom. Each baby's face, each additional as-
pect of her firstborn's personality. And with each first
expression, each fresh wonder in Michael's eyes, each
new discovery, Doris drowns another baby face below.*

*Fantasy. Stupidity. A vulgar bent to the darkness of
her own ungodliness much simpler, more complete, and
quite the opposite of dead.*

*Except for Silas, and then but a boy, none of the
current Kingstons have ever seen pier or wharf or
any boats come and gone; and not even Silas—who
aged-four watched the last rotting logs of the tumble-
down wharf house swept away by the hurricane of September 1947—only Silas knows that, beneath the surface, carved lengthwise into those piles, are a stack of
letters running down the first cypress trunk:*
t-h-e l-o-r-d g-i-v-e-t-h
A stack of letters running to the bottom with the other:
t-h-e w-a-t-e-r s-h-o-w-e-t-h f-o-r-t-h
*Unknown and unseen, those words—mystical as mer-
maids, tragic as dead babies—remain. Mottos are meant
to be proclaimed: written on a seal, a banner, on a coin;*

a shield, or on a plaque above gate/door/hearth. But sunken in dark water forever out of sight?

Curse over christening. Sin offering over baptism.

And with sinful families (as with institutions), each generation strives to legitimize their distinguishing iniquities to ease the wickedness bequeathed and undertaken by the next. The necessity for morality. These families strive to create a system of life that cheats sin. Pre-loads it with—if not absolution—legal justification and social acceptance for their worst misdeeds' acceptable continuation.

OF THE TWELVE GENERATIONS from the original Kingston brothers to the individual prowling from the North Vista Outhouse in the pre-dawn dark, Silas Kingston was the sixth to carry the patriarchal name, and with it, the titular responsibility for the familial corruption that reached from the past to embrace Foxtail Farm and hold him in its grip. A fist that reminded him—were one to accept the word of God as expressed in the Book of Job 1:21—that no one escapes the takings away of the Lord.

Long ago, Silas had made this truth his own, and he would live/die with that foremost of his burdens.

He passed the long, narrow pitch of grass mowed between the estate wall and the family chapel. In the spring and in the summer, shaded by the pine trees that shielded Foxtail Farm from the semi-private lane outside the property, this patch of lawn proved useful for badminton, volleyball, croquet. More peaceful competitions than the duel with pistols that ensured Foxtail Farm's carrying name would be Silas rather than Judah.

Silas often wondered if, as the story went, upon claiming the contested bride for himself, the original Silas Kingston had loved her as much as he had loved Doris. Did true love thrive from an original sin or was love merely that sin's prisoner until death?

Silas contemplated love and sin, and which dies last, the duration of his drive to the J. Edgar Hoover Building, headquarters of the FBI at 935 Pennsylvania Avenue in northwest Washington, D.C. There to confess to FBI counterintelligence his career-long treason against the United States, perhaps it was appropriate that he found parking alongside Ford's Theater.

Here, like the original Silas to his brother Judah, John Wilkes Booth had shot President Lincoln from behind. As with both murders, it wasn't about a woman at all, but about the regrettable necessity of Virginia's "peculiar institution." And when the canvas hood whipped over his head, Silas Kingston knew the surprise both men had felt. The inevitability of it all. But of the three, only Silas offered back a fuck-you/fuck-me face to fate.

Tuesday, July Sixth
1.

THE GREEN BOARDS OF its covers are heavier, and there are no pages for a record of comings and goings, but the "retired" CIA credential is, in size and shape, like a US passport. Opened, as it was now in front of the nose of the D.C. Metro patrol officer stationed on a swivel stool outside the medical/surgical unit doors on the fourth floor of George Washington University Hospital, the cop read the watermark inside the diagonal pink stripe through the picture bio-page.

"Says you're retired."

"From the CIA. Yes. That is correct." The late middle-aged man, off the elevator at 1:50 a.m., offered nothing else. Waited.

"Why would they send you?"

"No one sent me."

Waited again.

"And you want inside?"

He watched the cop's eyes dilate. Adrenaline hit.

"You got a partner?" said the man.

The cop lay his newspaper aside. Rose from his seat. "I'm going to ask you to—"

"Don't. That's my partner in there—the woman with the throat wound. Because I aged-out into my pension six months ago, I wasn't with Lynn—Ms. Kingston—at the airport last night."

The man's dark eyes narrowed, discerning. Like that, the cop's notional threat negated. His hormone surge accelerated sympathy rather than aggression.

"I'd like to sit with her through the dark part of the night. If she goes, she's going to have me beside her. She doesn't have anyone else. And, no, this isn't official. I assume you have a partner?"

The police officer dipped his chin.

"Then you understand how personal this might be." The retired CIA officer shifted his eyes to the door windows. "For her." He knew he had him but goosed it, anyway. "She's a victim, not the perp."

"Awful. This terrorism we gotta live with. People have no idea how bad it really is, but—what am I telling you? Room four-oh-eight."

The patrol officer deactivated the door lock. The CIA man gave him a wink. A crooked smile. Indicated the folded *Washington Post*. Ascribed a line in the air with his index finger. "Fifteen across is kind of a clever cheat. Once you get it, it unlocks the whole thing." With that, Russell Aiken passed inside.

♛ ♛ ♛

RETIRED. REMOVED. Disconnected from anything remotely related to KALEIDOSCOPE. Except for Lynn Kingston. Some facet of it, some refraction of its twisted light, briefly taking shape, had attempted to kill her. Kill her brother. Had killed Michael Kingston's cut-out.

Kalaydoskop? KALEIDOSCOPE? Silas Kingston?

Russell Aiken wouldn't put it past him, but, more likely, this was the work of other players now that the old man was out of its circle. Aiken knew one thing about it—*all* parties involved maintained tripwires invisible and deadly.

Nathan Muir to Tom Bishop to me: "'What makes them most dangerous is they operate in a reality we don't perceive.' The exposure of one threatens the exposure of both."

Face pale. An air tube ran to one nostril, the other nostril unrestricted. Her mouth was closed, her lips dry. Colorless. Lynn's auburn hair, back from her face. Some spilled, limp and unwashed, from behind her simple ears, from behind the almost childlike curve of her neck where it met her unblemished shoulders.

A tracheostomy tube rested in situ at the base of her heavily bandaged throat.

Aiken watched her vitals for the better portion of two hours. As they ran steady, he hadn't bothered to figure them out. He'd squeezed her hand—each arm restrained to the bedframe—every few minutes since he'd arrived. Whispered her name in her ear. She showed zero indication of consciousness. He was coming to the end of the two hours he'd allotted himself as a safe window for his visit.

He hadn't expected she'd be waiting to receive him, chipper and bright, and as only a conduit for her brother Michael—another Nathan Muir jack-in-the-box protocol triggered, but unused, a decade ago at the old spymaster's death—Aiken operated on little more information than either sibling; but what little he knew, he knew Lynn would want. Would need. And his last orders—

Nathan Muir to Tom Bishop to me: "The greatest fight facing the Agency won't be ours... It will belong to another. She must be protected. Shield her until she's ready to take it all apart." And I've already failed at that. Almost fatally.

A single piece of information he needed to share with her. To help her. Help her brother. To keep them out of step from the next set of tripwires. But it was three minutes to 4:00 a.m. He wouldn't press his luck. Trigger something else.

He took her hand. He leaned in, lips brushing her ear. "It's Russell, again. I have to go, but I'll be back. I know you will, but keep my visit in confidence."

He straightened his back but, for a moment, couldn't release her hand as his heart filled with a surge of sorrow and regret. He leaned over again. Placed his lips on her forehead and kissed. Aiken didn't whisper, this time, when he said, "I am so sorry, Lynn. For everything—"

⚜ ⚜ ⚜

"—I really am."

A voice. (His voice?)

I'm hurt... I'm HURT, but I'm alive. I must be.

Lynn tried to squeeze his hand. Her hand flexed. Barely.

Feel me?

The pressure of his hand increased.

"Lynn, can you open your eyes? Are you awake?"

I'm awake.

Her eyes scanned behind their lids. Lids twitched but did not part.

Wake up, Lynn! It's him!

Her entire being, cocooned in a feelingless haze, pulsed with something like a memory of deep sadness, of feelings she could name, but couldn't connect with, and the haze became magnetic, pulling her deeper into its layers.

No. Rise to his voice. Fight this. You must tell him.

(Relax, it only needs to be a dream. Release, relax, let go.)

(Fight?) Fight!

Her eyes fluttered with more energy. Russell Aiken moved his mouth closer to her ear.

"It's only one thing. A simple thing. You're going to hold on to it. Remember it."

He clenched her hand. Relaxed his grip. Her fingers twitched. Her eyelids twitched. Eyeballs raked. Back and forth.

"Stay here. Grip my hand as hard as you can, grip my voice, and listen. 'Gladys. Sent.' All you need to know. 'Gladys. Sent.'"

Tell him, Lynn! Tell him!

But air didn't make it past her throat.

Dulles. The scissors. Michael. (Not that—TELL HIM!)

Her chest convulsed. Air blew through the valve at the base of her neck. Oscillated. Out/in-out/in-out/in. She bucked her shoulders. Aiken forced her still.

"You have a tracheostomy, Lynn. It's temporary. Take it easy. We don't want nurses. I just—Need. You. To. Listen."

Calm-calm-Lynn. Calm.

"There-you-go."

He beheld her. Anguish, regret, deepened the lines in his face. He'd let her make her first move, blind and alone.

Her eyes popped wide. Darting. Panicked. More focused inward than out. Her pulse and blood pressure continued at an elevated rate.

"You're going to blink to show you understand me. Blink." He rushed. Commanded.

Shadows. Can't see his face. Weird light. No focus.

"Blink. Do it."

Blink. Tell him. Tell him who we are. Blink. Us—two plus one, all three. Most secret alive precious between us. And it just took the one time—isn't that funny? Blink!

Lynn did not blink. Her mouth twitched, the white-crust corners of chapped and swollen lips trying to find definition—

"Jesus. You can't be serious."

—in a smile.

"It's the meds—I know. You're high. But you got it. *Please* blink: 'Gladys-sent.'"

Muir secretary. Jessie nanny/grandma. Gladys. Bli-iink.

Lynn Kingston blinked her eyes. Aiken *fuck-yeah* clenched his jaw. Her hand. Her vitals spiked harder. "Just one other thing. For now."

Rusty: She's ours! That one time. I'm so-so-so-sorry.

"Michael is alive. He met a cut-out in Greece. The cut-out took the bullet at Dulles. Not Michael. I don't know what he knows, but I think Michael understands. The only way to the center of the thing is by defining the edge. Trust him—even when he doesn't trust himself or want you to."

Whir. The oxycodone drip cycled.

Haze. Haze-hands. Pulling. Tugging. Magnetic.

(Scissors. Stupid-bitch-scissors.)

Not awake. Not real. He can't be/wasn't. God doesn't love me.

(Why did you ask me that, Silas? My own mother.)

My toes curl in crushed seashell river-sand-muck. Looking up, looking out. See the mermaids—smooth cypress faces—river-running-water fingers through thick green hair; hear them calling, "Linny-Lynn-Lynn. Dive under so deep, so thick, so welcome, swim with us!"

"Don't cry."

He cups my face. Warm hand. Cold cheek. Wet.

Aiken thumbed away her tears.

Why couldn't you choose me?

The sound of a warning alarm. A nurse's station somewhere beyond the door.

Ten years—Parents—what's he saying...?

"...have your back—and I'll do better—but you cannot contact me in any form or fashion. KALEIDOSCOPE has tripwires neither of us can see."

Shut up, Rusty! Shut-up-I-don't-care! She's yours! She's ours!

Tears rolled, but the drugs had eased her calm. Aiken released her hand. "If anyone can pick the lock, it's Michael."

Hand gone. Warm gone.

Leigh gone.

The sound of movement. A flash of dim light with the movement of her door.

Rusty gone.

And, as the green mermaids pulled out of the wakening cocoon, and beneath the dead surface of the river of darkness inside of her, conscious/conscience drowned with—

I betrayed all three of us to Silas.

    ♛♛♛

SOME STRONG MATCHES the Kingston threw at the night to celebrate their rebellion from the Crown Clive Lancer served. Those military illumination rounds, as peculiar—certainly extra-legal—a touch as they were, Clive had to admit: the Kingston fireworks show was an exhilaration.

"Want to bang one, Clive? There's nothing to it," the soldier son, Hal, holds out a bomb to him. Although he's passed a light infantry course in his training evals and easily remembers his way around a mortar, Clive doesn't want to show that up. Especially under Silas's raptor's gaze.

Paige, embarrassed, takes it off his hands. "You said it was my night to learn something new." She drops and lobs it.

The ka-rump times to her dishy, lairy mom, edging beside him. Gwen whispers in Clive's ear— "In this family, that's what we call 'popping your cherry-bomb.'"

"What was your take on the old man?" Fergus asked.

"Outside the normal paternal suspicion of an outsider lighting up his granddaughter?"

"Anything else?"

"I perceived him preoccupied with something beyond the holiday. I'll give you that."

"We *know* that."

"Scooted off in a bit of hurry not long after."

"How long?"

"No more than an hour."

"And the soldier-son?"

"Rather friendly chap. Favorite of the little ones—"

"He's a killer. Don't forget it."

"He doesn't hide it. It's stamped on his skin."

Fergus's feral eyes burned. Did an almost undetectable quivery thing. Particularly unfriendly. Particularly unamused.

"Military tattoos. Scars," Clive added.

Clive's true opinion of Hal—based on their brief interaction—was an openness, an innocence of place and purpose, a happiness with life and an eagerness to please. Clive liked Hal. Liked him quite a bit. Envied, in a small way, the sort of pure fool who takes the world as it comes and knows no other path but ride headlong, spear level, to justice.

"A bad'un to be sure," Fergus grunted. Indicated a short stack of folders on the motel table. "Brush up on the lot of 'em. Our focus is Silas. Getting you close to him. And if it's not the girl—"

"Why wouldn't it be?"

"We'll get to that."

After having left Foxtail Farm in the earliest hours of the fifth of July, Clive Lancer drove sixteen miles to the Super 8 on Route 235, where his team leader, cover name Fergus Jones, had booked him a room in the three-story motor inn. Fergus passed him the profile dossiers—dossiers he'd read enough times not to forget a single detail—none of which ("bravo" Legoland on the Thames) got near-at-all to the hearts or minds of the people he'd met. Fergus gave him the room key. Briefed him his cover— "You're taking a college sabbatical—" that Clive would need to retool to match the cover he'd already blown. The Scotsman instructed him to text Paige a "Thank you" midday on the fifth and, if uninvited, show up and surprise the lass on the sixth.

The Scotsman at the door, and Clive: "What did you mean 'We'll get to that?'"

"Don't like being played. Don't believe your story—how you met. Don't like not saying so to Vauxhall to get you approval to get your dick wet—"

"Hey. Wait a minute."

Fergus slammed his forearm across Clive's chest, jamming him into the doorframe. "No, you wait a minute." Hot-hissed in his face. "You think you fool me, mate? You've been excess baggage on this op all summer. Here on someone else's hopes this'd shake you out of our tree, get you to put in papers."

Too far. Fergus backed off. Snorted. Looked at the parking lot.

"I love my job."

"Don't take the piss. Every three years they send me a duffer they're afraid'll make a dog's dinner out of anything else." Only now did he meet Clive's gaze. "They do it 'cause they don't know like I know who and what Silas Kingston is. Was. Always will be, and how he's going to pay for it."

"Anytime you want to tell me…"

"I have never been this close, young squire. Maybe you and the twat—your convergence—will do me right. For once. Any event, I covered for you. Made you look everything but the fuck-up you are. Said this was all your spur of the moment idea last night—even though I know you've been listening to her recordings; know you went yesterday a'sniffin' after her like the randy dog you are. But you bang her, you bang her for Queen and Country."

"She's seventeen. That's rape in this country."

"So you'll wait six days till her birthday. Then, like the gentleman said, it's 'Close your eyes, think of England, and pull the trigger.' By then, she should be dripping for you."

Clive braced. Thought twice. "What's not to love, a job good as that?"

"Thatsa lad. Throw some of your black magic on her. We want her eating out of your hand. You're going to get her so cross-eyed, boy, she'll do whatever we want." He poked Clive's shoulder. "You get the girl, and you get to keep your job right alongside *this* ol' duffer who's gonna come out a hero."

Fergus left. Went back to the Listening Post at Garde-Joyeuse. Clive cursed him but did as he asked the next day—the text, waited for a call, a *ding* back, anything.

Nothing.

Now, here, edge of the bed on the sixth, worked out, fed and full, spiffed up, and read-in for the umpteenth time on the Kingston clan, forgot about cursing him at all as he counted the hours till he'd hold Paige once more in his arms.

What the hell, anyway? Fergus was right about Clive Lancer.

One foot out the door when he'd arrived in the States, discovering Paige—unaccustomed feelings he couldn't/wouldn't deny—changed that. Changed Queen-and-everything-country about it.

Midnight moon. High moon. Glimmering moon, running river surface, heavenly fire. A beach walk like they were born to it. Fingers. Alternating dark/light, dark/light, born and grown to this fixed-point-in-the-universe moment's perfect fit. Perfect thumb. Soft on thumbnail. Light on dark.

Silver moonlight. Black water. Meeting eyes and matching looks.

Lips as questions. Joined as answers.

"No. Wait. Stop it—Not you. Me." Paige.

(Stopping. Puzzled.)

"I don't know, Clive. I can't. I'm so—" Throaty growled disappointment. "Wait. I can-I-just-wasn't—I do. Kiss me? Start over? Lemme kiss you?"

He let the moment pass. Whatever would happen between him and Paige, he would not calculate/weigh/measure/mask. No. That was everything else he'd ever done. Buying the judgment of others but never himself.

Whatever Silas Kingston might have colluded on with the Russians, CIA never admitted it to the SIS, didn't seem to care, and probably wouldn't take kindly to old Fergus rubbing their noses in it.

"RED, WHITE, AND BLUEBERRY pancakes!" Hal called from the kitchen. "Get 'em while the gettin's good!"

Little Silas came thumping down the stairs, sliding onto the landing bend, careening around his mom, who was adjusting Jack's— "Too tight! I don't like it!"—bathing suit, hollered back, "What's the red?"

"Your milk!"

And, thumping on down, "The milk's the white!" Little Silas charged from sight.

"Mom, I need a new one." Jack.

Melody. "You are growing like a sunflower this summer."

"Red's the batter—ask your mom how—just come on, I wanna get down to the beach!"

Melody tweaked threads in the elastic waistband. "Hold still." And Jack did. "They're red velvet, like the muffins you like," she added, absently, her mind straying to thoughts of Silas.

His *I'll be back soon* note she'd found sticking from the screen door. *Don't worry—S.K.*

You don't write "don't worry" unless you think I'm going to...and care that I shouldn't when I do.

The tremor ran through her. The tremor she didn't like. The tremor she always felt with her father when he'd go off. Hadn't felt it since her father went inside. But before that—the robberies or blackmail or swindle or hijack—this, with Silas, was that same damn shiver-and-twitch.

She snipped a thread with a thumbnail. "One more should do it."

Little Silas and Hal laughed in the kitchen. Jack didn't move. She glanced up at him. He gazed at his grandmother's portrait.

"B-O-O-N-E," Jack said. "Why does it say 'bone' on Gramma Doris's picture?"

Her eyes followed his finger to the artist's signature.

"Painting."

"Painting."

"Bone has one 'O.' B-o-n-e. Two O's is an *ew* sound. Buh-ew-nnn."

Grin. "Like Daniel Boone? My Fourth of July costume name? On a pic—on a painting?"

"Not *Daniel* Boone. It's another Boone." She laughed. "Boone is the name of the artist who painted the portrait."

"Painting."

"Yes. And when it's a painting of a person, it's a portrait. Boone was a painter who painted portraits."

"Was Boone his whole name?"

"Could be *his*. Could be a *hers*. It could be a first name, like Jack, or a last name, like Kingston. We'll never know," she lied.

Jack scrunched his face. Melody reached up and put her finger over the last two letters. "Cover it like this, it's *BOO!* Like a ghost."

Jack giggled. "I'm hungry."

"Me too," said Melody, smiling and curious. Like Doris's portrait. Lifelike eyes following their descent. And then they were gone. *Boo.*

"THREE STEPS away from me. One-two-three and turn around fast, and say, 'Boo!'"

Doris and Boone. A sketch session. Foxtail Farm, upstairs morning room. Doris takes three dramatic strides away from the artist. Whirls. "Boo!"

"And hold." His charcoal glides across the large Bristol pad in his lap. "And do it again."

"Boo."

"And hooold it."

She bathes in vivid sunlight that pours through the floor-to-ceiling arched window.

He flips his page. Works a rapid-fire series. Detailed versions of her mouth. "What kind of panties you say you're wearing under that dress?"

"I'm sor—?"

"Don't speak. I don't want to hear it. There. That thought. And walk again: one-two-three, Boo. Panties?"

The "oo" pout; the feisty humor in her eyes.

"A Polaroid camera might get the look you want in fewer tries."

"I don't want that look. That's your look. I want my instant memory of your look. That's my look. That's what your dear Mr. Kingston is paying me for. Oh, by the way—one, two, three, go, go—do you give it to your husband, or do you just lie there?"

Walk/turn/boo— "Is this the day the artist attempts to seduce his subject?"

"Puh-lease, Doris."

Doris pinches the hem of her sundress. Sudden flash. No panties.

"Now, that's disgusting," says Boone.

Doris: horror, embarrassment, gone-too-far shame.

Boone grins. She snorts in relief.

"Yes! THAT!" He captures it in charcoal. Blows black ash. Scrawls another. "Say, 'Boo!'"

Doris takes three steps. Spins. Kisses the air.

Freeze the moment.

This is the moment Boone will trap in rich, red-oil lips. Trap eyes: dark blue, highlighted with diamond cerulean crypts, kaleidoscope-patterned, vivid, confident. The wished-for look he sought to make his, living/alive when he moved on her and she rejected him. The eyes he realized in the finished portrait weren't entirely hers.

(Melody knows.)

The hidden torment that faces the viewer, faces him—that night after that day—from the medicine cabinet mirror over the yellow-stained sink. His cramped, dirty bathroom. The reek of turpentine splashed by shaking hands into the bowl and down the drain. He studies the mirror. Life's reflection. The horror opposite of art. He decided then. He would complete the portrait. He would drink champagne with proud, preening Silas and untouchable Doris, complicated in onion layers of joy and tragedy, sweetness, bitterness, a full, fluid heart protected by a paper-thin skin that would take only a pinch to crumble, flake and fall away. Then he would do this thing at home he knew he must.

His eyes: torment and pain. Her eyes: joy and tragedy. Boone's lust for her is a thin disguise for the true love that he ignored/squandered/lost. Would destroy. Doris Kingston, unlike anyone else he's ever painted, will be his last portrait. He knows that. He swallows. They'll remember me. Vile beer/bourbon/turpentine. Every damn everyone. Doris absorbs him and he sees the eyes he will paint. Sees the murder he will commit. Doris Kingston, unlike anyone else he's ever painted, will be his last portrait. He knows that. He swallows.

♔ ♔ ♔

"MOM SAYS Daniel Boone painted Grandma Doris's painting."

"He'd a'hadta to be a ghost to do it," Hal chuckled. Poured syrup. Met his wife's eyes.

A winsome smile. "I think I'll buy the boys new swimsuits this week."

"Mom, did you ever see a ghost?" Little Silas. Red velvet teeth.

"You know we don't talk when our mouths are full."

Hal gave the boy a fake cuff on the back of his head. Said to Melody: "Good idea. The bathing suits. Go for it."

"And outfits—not matching, don't freak—if I can find anything. For Paige's birthday."

The boys and their dad concocted a plan for a sand castle with army men and dinosaurs they would mine with leftover firecrackers— "And film it?" "You bet 'and film it'"—as soon as they got down to the sand.

Melody thought again about Silas's disappearance, his irksome note, while on the landing, an odd air current caught the threads Melody dropped loosening Jack's ill-fitting swimsuit. Suspended in the air, they *whooshed* through the banister rail and away.

FREAKIN' STUPID. Freaking teeny bopper, like an I've-never-been-kissed freakazoid kid.

I wanted the kiss. I wanted to kiss him. I wanted him to kiss me. Why'd I freak out? What he must be thinking now. God-you-blew-it-Paige. Stupid.

Deeb. The sand piles beyond the bonfire; forcing himself onto me. His gunk, sticky with sand, on my knee after Clive left. I-go-all-frigid. Fuckin' gross. Asshole.

(Why then? *The one guy I* want *to kiss me. Why'd I think of that? Feel what wasn't there as if it burned my leg.)*

"Iced tea...? Paige?" Aunt Melody.

"What?" Melody wagged a blue and yellow beverage can. "Uh. No. Thanks. I'm good."

Melody cocked her head. A funny look. Suspected Paige was not "good"; her look invited conversation. Paige rose. Walked to the water.

Near the tree trunk drift log, sapwood sun-bleached white and wind/sand fuzzed. Near where she'd made her epic fail.

They'd laughed on their way there. Whatever they talked about that night, they saw the same funny side to it. A young man—almost her age, or she almost his—seeming older because of the secrets. Things he couldn't tell her, wouldn't say, were *comfortable* for her.

The whole of life she'd grown up around, now with someone to share the dynamic on equal terms. Was that more attractive than the movie-star-spy-to-die-for looks?

God, his jaw, those shoulders. That smile.

They'd found plenty of things, normal things, things they laughed about.

Mom and Dad, did they have that before all this?

"I know you dig country, but just so there's no problem on the go-forward, I'm strictly a classical man."

"Classical music?"

"Strictly."

Coming down the rickety wooden stairs after Melody gathered the twins, and her mother winked goodnight at Clive (more than her), "Bedtime, kids," and Hal filled in the trench. Aunt Linny gone, and Papa nowhere to be found. Let me show you our beach.

"You're kidding me with the violins, right?"

"And the harp and bassoon 'nnn-yeeess. I mean, I like it, but..."

Paige laughed when he aptly called the new fad-sound "Hick-Hop" coming out of Nashville, which they both agreed needed to die a quick and painful death. He admitted, where he came from, a dose of country music was, more often than not, *Sweet Home Alabama* karaoke'd loud and pissed by a bunch of sweaty prats, followed up by *Save a Horse Ride a Cowboy* and someone or all of them falling off the stage.

"Is there always a stage?"

"No, sometimes they fall right off the flat earth. But I downloaded some of your Rascal Flatts."

"And?"

"Too high for my karaoke voice."

She asked when Brits shot off fireworks and he replied, "Guy Fawkes Day. November fifth is our Bonfire Night."

"You do bonfires?"

"In public. More when I was a kid. There'd be competitions, entire neighborhoods would toss in their junk. Not so much anymore. Everyone's gotten a little nanny-ish about it all."

They walked along the river's edge to the curve in the shore where the wharf and trading post and dock once stood. "What are those two green things out there? Look like...heads or something."

They'd run out of the room where the sand ran out. Paige laughed. Leaned into him. It seemed so natural to do and she laughed and she said, "My Aunt Linny's mermaids. C'mon, let's go the other way."

He took her arm. "I'm not ready to go back up."

She gave him a sly look. "Aren-chu? Mmm..." a purr and she tossed her hair and ran on sea-fairy tip toes, turning a time or two to kick water at him, until she let him catch up. She wasn't cold when she snuggled into his chest, his arm around her, and they walked past the driftwood trunk where the bluffs rose higher and higher, and closed in, shortening the shore. And when Paige asked Clive why he'd chosen to become a spy, he'd told her he hadn't. He'd taken a foreign service exam, and they put the moves on him from there.

"When I figured out what we were getting to, it seemed cool, so I seduced them right back."

"You're good at that." Head on his shoulder.

"Too good for my own good."

Enquiring eyes rose to his wink. Paige said, "You've lost sight of your mission?"

That stopped him. A bit jarred. A bit of a *what the hell* chuckle. "I'd almost forgotten who you are."

"A regular Mata Hari. Been hearing about 'the mission' since I first remember hearing."

They laughed; he liked that one too.

As the bank shortened, they waded foot-deep in the water. Paige wasn't ready to turn around. What that might lead to—the excitement creepy-crawling her skin—too delicious. Clive stopped. He took both her hands, his dry, warm palms sliding down until only their fingertips linked.

"I've already told you way too much. I won't tell you much more. But I know that you, of all people, will understand this last bit."

The security of total happiness and newfound trust beamed from her face, and she could see something in Clive, looking right back at her, that carried a quality unlike any look any boy, man, or anyone had ever shown back at her.

"Let's keep walking?" she said, and they did, and he said: "It's the old chestnut about bangers— 'it's better not to see what goes inside them'? I work in the 'better not see' part of the kitchen. I signed up for that. Just turns out, I'm not terribly keen on bangers even when they're served. I've wanted to tell you—since even before I spoke to you—to tell *you*. I think I'm done."

"Are you quitting? Do they even let you? They must reel you back in and don't let you walk moonlight beaches with American girls whose grandpas you've been trying to trap."

They arrived back at the white driftwood tree trunk. This time they stopped. They cradled hands and Paige couldn't remember when they'd started, but their fingers, perfectly laced, made him easy to pull, gently, down beside her. Her imagination of what might be catching up rocket-fast to what already is, and she was thinking about kissing him, but heard herself saying, "Here's what I think's dumb. If you keep coming here to spy and keep going home with nothing but keep coming back—because someone *really* thinks there's something."

She watched her hand slide up his cheek.

"They're never going to let Papa quit. He's always going for 'tune-ups'—Dad calls 'em the same thing and I'm not stupid. Don't you think—?"

One hand went around the back of his head. The other held his face in her palm.

Softer than the lap of the river on the sand: "Don't you think our side might already know? Might not even care. Might not appreciate you snooping around?"

His hands slid around her waist. Paige nestled into them. Allowed him to draw her closer.

"Never did before just now. I'm not even cleared for what I'm supposed to be looking for."

"The bigger it is, the more likely the CIA would know—" her voice left her, her eyes closed, her lips parted and the two of them joined warm and soft and—

And Deeb attacked me all over again. Couldn't do it. Just for a second. Stammered/begged/proved myself an idiot.

A call with a "Thank you for having me" VM the next day. A pussy "Can I come see you?" text yesterday at school. Just come over, but why-would-he? Why even bother? You don't live around here—like around this whole country, and—

"Paige!"

Ugh. What is with Melody today?

"You just going to ignore your friend?"

Did Mom just mutter into her hard lemonade: "I'll take him?"

Paige turned and had to take a step backward because—big, broad smile—Clive was moving fast and laughing. Monster hands up and causing Leigh and the twins to giggle because Paige was stumbling, losing her balance, half-laughing/half-screaming. Charlotte blushing and self-consciously wrapping in her towel and—

"What're you doing, you freak?!"

She splashed to her butt. He extended his hand.

"I thought about what we talked about?"

"I don't remember what we talked about." She splashed him.

"My job. I said something. You know, put in a request."

"What are you talking about?"

"They've allowed me a sabbatical."

Until that moment, Paige had lived without knowing that her heart could scream inside her. "You're staying here?"

"Lexington Park. Room at the—"

"Don't bother. I'm never going there."

Quizzical look. Serious man.

"Your *room*. Go to Lexington all the time. My school's in Lexington."

Ehh. 'School.' Why'd I say that? Sound like a kid.

"I didn't know they had a university." He winked.

She splashed him again. "Oh, shut up. It's *hours* before I'm graduated."

He grinned. Splashed her back just to tease some more.

"Real mature."

"Paige is having a b-day on Sunday! Love to see you here!" Gwen.

Charlotte. "*Ew*-Mom."

Gwen peeled with laughter and lay back and stretched, cat-like in the sun.

Clive, lips to her ear, playing up the sexy voice. "I'm not invited?"

Paige pushed him away. Clive splashed onto his butt beside her. Only now did she extend her hand. "Help me up?"

He stood. He lifted her.

"One rule: if you're going to be hanging around, no more listening to my calls. Because I'm going to be talking about you."

Clive raised his hands in surrender. "Not I."

And technically, he wasn't lying.

"We say 'not me' around here."

"It's incorrect."

"You'll get used to it. Mate."

He cocked his head, marking her last word a double entendre.

Mate/sex... (Deeb tearing at my bathing suit.) Shut up, brain!

She shoved the cold rush down. Grinned right back and said, "Morgan is going to shit when I bring you."

"Bring me where?"

"They call it The Enchanted Forest, but I'll let you decide. Back here's gonna be cake and candles—Sunday-my-actual-birthday, but Saturday night, yeah—Morgan's throwing me a fantastic party. She'll be excited to see us together."

Morgan: You. Are. Gonna. Die. When you see me and him!

2.

S HOVED INTO A CHAIR. Snatch—unhooded. Snip—flex cuffs yanked, wrists free. Silas twisted them. Rubbed raw but not too bad. Checked his wristwatch. Nice to discover that at 4:30 p.m., his internal clock—mind-monitored in the darkness of hood-world—short only twenty minutes. Sensory deprived, better to slow your inner clock than speed up. A false-time speed-up, you're doing your abductors a favor driving yourself faster than you need to first stage, gut-punch, psychological loss of hope that most adult kidnap victims hit when they perceive they've passed the twenty-four-hour mark. Of course, some don't wait twenty-four. Perceived or otherwise. Crack in five or ten. Some crack so fast/hard/bust-up-completely they buy themselves a bonus beat-down or even a bullet that might not have ever been theirs for the taking. In Silas's case, his captors had held him thirty-three hours since the snatch from the Ford's Theater parking lot across from FBI Headquarters.

To what purpose? Performative. East-West dick-measuring. A butch dance between Silas Kingston/KALEIDOSCOPE and Nikoláj "Kolya" Yurenev/Kalaydoskop.

The two of them had been rubbing up against each other for thirty years.

Not that the dance wasn't deadly. Just that they needed to keep it going. The music playing. Musical chairs for over a century. The phantasmagoria tumbling round in the lens, until the picture—perfect, clear, definable—locked, doubtless. Until one of them and only one (other player-opponents need not apply; penalty of death), and the eleven decades of dual K/K operations would end. A sudden play. A single directive. A total capture-kill. A world irrevocably rearranged to one absolute advantage. Follow-up move, reversing event? Impossible in perpetuity. Turn and turn and turn the lens.

Forgivable, then, that Silas found his head-bagging trite. Only the Russian knew where he was going and had a reason to stop him. And for that matter, the kidnap props and stew—what's the point? He would have gotten a worse outcome from his own countrymen once he'd started talking. Silas: in it for keeps. His family: for keeps. A hood. A careening van. Zip restraints and lumpy, too narrow/too short love seat to fetal position on for thirty-plus hours: Amateur theatrics.

The one with ham-hands pinned his shoulders. Held Silas in the cheapo garage sale meet safe house chair. At a cheapo table for him to look across at black-out curtains and a digital A/V recorder—not cheapo at all—on a tripod. Black-eyed and staring.

In unaccented English behind him: "You'll not turn around. That would prove inconvenient as a life-choice."

Beyond the curtains, a large motorcycle engine revved. There had been hours of that all of yesterday afternoon. Followed by the occasional clank of tools. Just the one engine—so it wasn't a commercial garage—and, a little farther out, the slappity-slap of a basketball, shoe scuff and male grunt and unintelligible trash-talk. Game shouts. Between the basketball and the motorcycle engine work, Silas had listened to the chain-clanking activity of an electric parking gate, most active from around 4:30 to 7:00 yesterday afternoon. The same twelve hours later. People off to/home from work.

Safe house, next to a private house with a detached garage, next to an apartment complex with gated parking lot, next to a park. This was a one-off stash house Kolya didn't care about hiding. The toss of a doggie-bone if Silas was quick and KALEIDOSCOPE wanted to take out the temp-hires Kalaydoskop put up for this minor inconvenience. Sometimes we share.

Silas's eyes gleamed; the start of the game, always a treat.

A second set of hands slapped a cheapo cellular flip phone, fresh from its CVS packaging, in front of him.

"When this rings, you will answer it on speakerphone."

"And the camera? You sure Kalaydoskop wants to be recorded? Everyone voice-prints these days."

"He will only provide instructions pre- our recording of your response, old man."

Silas nodded once. "Okie-dokie."

He sat. Stared.

Motorcycle engine revs. Sputters out. Metal smack of tools. Foot scuffle, ball shuffle, chain rattle of the basketball net. Distant crow caws.

A carrion crow weathervane with a bone in its beak.

But the flip phone remained silent. Silas laid his hands on the table. Loose-skinned, woodgrain-fine wrinkles. Unrecognizable from the hands, strong, straight fingered and smooth that took the telephone from the barman/waiter's tray to answer the call that changed and cursed the Kingston family with his every act and compulsion that followed him from a long ago, cold and cloudy day inside the Soviet Union.

♕ ♕ ♕

BARRING ACCIDENTAL fatal poisoning, Silas Kingston will achieve the greatest triumph of his Agency career with the most successful Soviet military recruitment in Moscow Station's last eight years. The poisoning Silas fears has nothing to do with spy versus spy cloak and dagger madness. Everything to do with an article in the Komsomolskaya Pravda—*the youth/young adult edition of* Pravda, *official newspaper of the Central Committee of the Communist Party of the Soviet Union—that tucked away in a bottom corner of a "Of Local Interest" column between the sports and travel sections, an acknowledgement and a caution. In the third week of April (this, the first week of May), in the Northern Central Russian Upland, spring mushroom hunters had mistaken a poisonous fungi for the wild mushrooms gathered annually by Russians of the region for hun-*

dreds of years. Thirty citizens had perished, which, using the proper mathematical equation needed to compute Central Committee statistics, meant ninety to one hundred fatalities. Seated at a lunch table, tucked away from the sooty windows inside of the кафе/бар, ешьте нормально—*dubious in translation: the "Café/Bar Eat Fine"*—in the locomotive factory town of Yasnogorsk on the Vashana River outside of Tula, Silas smirks. His face and future focus on the pile of fried wild mushrooms, hot and greasy beside the minced pork and onion pelmeni dumplings dolloped generously with runny sour cream.

"Try, try. Picked fresh each morning. You will never have a better mushroom. I promise you, Mr. Pendry," says Colonel Bogdon Ogievich of the Soviet Air Force Long Range Aviation branch.

And maybe that's true because—if they are poison—he'll never have a mushroom or anything else again. Silas stretches his smile, digs in with his fork and eats a nice, healthy (hopefully "healthful") bite.

He doesn't die or retch or cramp or do anything other than enjoy this local delicacy—damn good mushrooms—and, the recruitment already made, this is their final face-to-face. Set their protocols. Go over their codes. Comms plan. And, if such a time arises, the colonel's exfiltration.

Then a telephone rings, and this isn't that. It never was.

Bogdon sits back. His face is passive. Active mental participation disengaged. He's observing Silas. Silas notices the ringing of the telephone growing louder as the barman/waiter carries it to them. No one is smiling anymore.

Silas stares at the ringing phone thrust past his shoulder. His face is drawn, but his hands do not shake as he allows the barman to put the ugliest orange, Soviet Bell Telephone rip off into their grip.

"It will ring until you answer, Silvanus Kingston."

👑👑👑

THE FACTORY RINGTONE played. Silas's fist clenched. Opened. Closed. Open, he seized the cheapo flip. Flipped it. Finger tapped the SPEAKER button. "All too dramatic and unnecessary for my taste—especially after so many years—but you have my attention."

"I think no more dramatic than your trip to the Hoover Building yesterday morning."

Silas said nothing. Didn't wait long before Kolya/Kalaydoskop baited him again. "Where one turns—"

"Save it. There isn't a version of that—"

"—the other corresponds."

"—where you don't end up dead when this is over."

"Mmm?"

"My children were off limits. Always. I kept *my* word."

"Children grow up."

Silas's lip curled at the smile he heard in the Russian's voice. "You know what's wrong with Russian comedy? Relies on clowns and none of you, beneath your greasepaint and rubber noses, are one bit funny."

"Ah, *Silvanus.* My martyred Bishop of Thessalonica—"

"'Silas,' you Godless prick."

"My faith is in this world. Mmm? And what would you have told the FBI about your lack of faith in yours, had I not stopped you....? As you intended."

"You moved on Michael. You know damn well—Everything."

"That, I'm afraid, is you assuming I am behind events in Turkey."

Silas propped his elbows on the table. Gathered his hands together. Leaned into his knuckles. "I'm waiting."

"An Orthodox priest and Greece in an economic death spiral. Turkey, their forever enemy. We do not operate inside a vacuum. Greece's debt crisis and recession threaten to spread across the EU."

"Brussels wasn't behind the events in Trabzon. They're weak. The best they got is the Nobel gold coin they're going to give themselves at the Oslo City Hall this December. The globalists have never coalesced in this as they would like."

"True and not true. They know and sometimes that is enough. But we will get to December."

"They're not a threat to you or to us," said Silas.

"'Us' now. You must find it difficult not saying 'me' any longer."

"My ego took its retirement right alongside *me*."

Kalaydoskop laughed. "Turkey wasn't *me*, which brings us back to my first remark: the lens is turning. If it isn't my hand and it isn't yours—also my hand—and yet a Kingston begins to dig—"

"Say his name," Silas snapped. "You know you want to. Michael Kingston!"

"You don't have to believe me, and don't—time will sort out the whole truth there—but you know this. You reached out, not I, because you need your hand on the kaleidoscope as much as I do."

Silas sighed. Silas leaned back in his chair, keeping his hands locked together in the appearance now of prayer. "Get to the camera."

"Same as the film we made after our very first conversation, so long ago."

Tula. Mushrooms. A Soviet phone, and "Call me Kalaydoskop."

Silas steepled his fingers. "What do you want me to provide you from the CIA?"

"Everything that pertains to that other event in December."

"The Baku Oil Conference."

"Yes," Kolya/Kalaydoskop, sighed. He barked a set of orders in Russian.

A small, black remote control over Silas's shoulder. Placed on the tabletop. Silas picked it up. "You'll wait," growled Ham-hands from behind.

Silas addressed the flip phone. "How does my confessing exactly what I'd planned to confess yesterday give you any advantage over me? You're wasting my time."

Silas dropped the remote. Hands on table. Pushed to his feet.

"Sit down!" Kalaydoskop barked.

Silas chuckled at the knowledge his case officer of thirty years had been watching him the whole time. He shook his head slowly, mocking the camera lens.

Kalaydoskop. Through the cheapo flip: "I can make you disappear, force you to watch as I make this *all* about Mi-chael."

Silas stiffened. Shoulders pinched. Back arching. Arms grabbed. Both sides. Shoved back into the chair. An old man filled with fear.

Kalaydoskop. Through the cheapo flip: "There will be no Kingston family when I'm finished with that nasty piece of business. Do not tempt me again."

Silas saw his reflection, small and warped in the camera's black eye. Saw a spasm in his cheek along his jaw.

Kalaydoskop. Through the cheapo flip: "Pick up the remote, Silas; now you may begin."

Silas watched his hand shaking, old and well into its final withering season, but exactly as he'd seen it in his prime. Tula. Taking the Soviet phone. The receiver against his ear—might as well have been a gun barrel, and Kolya's voice (the familiar name he'd known him by until that moment. Gracious, cultured, charming Kolya):

"Do you recognize this voice? Answer only 'Yes' or 'No.'"

"Yes."

"From this moment on, you are to refer to me only as Kalaydoskop."

"Yes."

"The next voice you will identify. Only 'Yes' or 'No.'"

Rough static. The cheapo receiver at the other end, moved. Repositioned near another mouth. Lips you only see once in your life and look to kiss forever. A panting, a whimper, a gut-deep cry of pain.

Silas says "Yes," recognizing the voice inside the wracking sob as that of his young wife, pregnant Doris, in agony.

3.

A FTER AN ENTIRE DAY hunting for the perfect hidey hole, two handmade signs, drawn in thick black marker, had drawn Michael Kingston's attention. Caused him to linger at the window on the Rue de la Survette long enough that proprietress, Helene Favre lifted faded gray eyes from the alterations table where she spent all her lonely days, to the mirror, black-rimmed/black-spotted from foxing. Caught his eye. Scowled at his drawn and damaged features. He gave her a smile. With a brusque wave of her darning needle, she drew him inside as if Michael had kept her waiting half her life.

"The sign in your window says, 'Internet Services'?" He tried her in English.

"Above the door it says 'Laundrenet' which backs that up nicely." She responded the same.

She didn't move from her seat. He approached her.

"I thought that was French for 'laundromat.'"

She didn't turn. "Do you read French?" She worked her needle.

"No."

"Then why would you think you could?"

Michael gaped at the back of her head. Silky gray hair—gobs of it, by the look—pinned and trussed in a tight swirl, fashionable in the earliest parts of the previous century. The old woman sewed. Didn't look like she was joking. The style of humor Michael liked most. He tried to catch her eye in the glass, smiling more broadly this time. Helene Favre remained impervious. "So," he said, "you're in the laundry *and* the internet business."

"I am, sir, in the moth business."

Michael could talk to anyone. Always found something to say. "I know that I don't know what that means. Does anyone?"

She held up the trousers to a man's worsted wool suit she had been reweaving. "Holes."

Michael caught her pixieish smirk in the foggy glass, where she met his gaze once more. Raised a fine, perfectly penciled eyebrow. Another round?

Michael said, "My father would tell me never to eat the holes in Swiss cheese."

Helene said, "The holes are where the nourishment resides; how we live so long in the cantons."

"But, ma'am—"

"Mrs. Favre, if you please."

"May I say, Mrs. Favre, you don't look a day over one hundred."

Earned himself a chuckle. "And people say Americans are dull. The men without romance."

"Romance is dead."

"I'm certainly not." She added, "Did you fall asleep in a garden?"

"Why?"

"Because your face looks like a lawnmower awakened you."

His bruised and wounded face, coupled with exhaustion, had done the exact opposite in improving his looks. "Funny you should say that. That's exactly how this happened."

Helene gave an unladylike snort. She remarked, since he didn't have clothing to mend, he was there to rent an internet station. Yes, he was, and he paid for the day in cash. Escape kit money he'd exchanged for Swiss francs still in his hand, he inquired about the second sign.

"Yes, the office room is available. You'll share it with a mop, so I will ask you don't talk its ear off."

"Does rent pay for 24-hour access?"

"Are you on the run from the law?"

"That is not who I am trying to avoid. No, Mrs. Favre." She pulled bills from his cash fan. "There is also a cot."

"Mrs. Favre, that would be enough for two weeks, and I don't plan—"

"You are my guest now, so it will be Helene. We shall settle the difference if and when I see you go."

♛♛♛

PELL & GLATISANT Trading. So damn familiar. So damn Kingston, in a way, but Michael couldn't pinpoint a memory. Nothing special about Michael's tradecraft. Two of Father Cevik's photographs had led him here. Shot on different days. One: snowy winter. One: late spring, maybe summer. A muffler'd Kalaydoskop, Van Dyke facial hair, surveilled camera-surveilling the

Pell/Glatisant fortress from inside a car. Cleanshaven Kalaydoskop in tourist togs, sandals—gets map directions from the doorman. A more studied look at the first, through snowfall: P/G in a lighted sign jutting off the corner turret; the bank's emblem—a mythical creature, half-serpent/half-leopard, *Genève – Anno 1973* in gold leaf upon the door glass.

On the run. Running fast. Pell & Glatisant Trading Conglomerate, GmbH, Geneva: the easiest edge from which to aim at the middle. The bullseye. Kalaydoskop. Cevik put the dart in his hand and Michael made his most confident throw. But who had hung the dartboard?

Unless I'm as stupid as Lynn constantly drives home with me, those two photos were the easiest, most obvious clue. Dangled right in front of my nose.

Whomever had assembled the photo-intel packet had wanted Michael here. Now. Well, if they wanted to watch Michael as they'd been watching Kalaydoskop, they hadn't/weren't finding him here: the fifth of five cubicles in a linty corner of a Swiss internet/launderette.

Pell & Glatisant Trading Conglomerate. The name buzzed Michael's imagination. Bugged him. Couldn't help but think it had something to do with his father. Was personal to his family. But the more he keyboard surfed and searched and studied: couldn't swat the fly.

No client scandals, no regulatory violations, no board of directors power plays. There were no trumpeted triumphs or mergers or acquisitions. Nothing overtly Russian—oligarch ties—nothing overtly high-flying lords of easy money, military-industrial complex American. A very private, very quiet place of money. A place of power. The quiet power that is behind every clandestine op.

The fuel that runs the engine of every spy game/every service.

Michael leaned back in his chair. Took a breather. Looked around.

"Don't get many customers."

"Swiss are clean people. *Sans autres.*"

Michael's fingers danced on the keys: *sans autres expression meaning... "Obviously."* Helene's continued stare in the mirror said as much. Michael said, "You wouldn't happen to have any coffee?"

"Whatever is in the vending machines."

Visible from his seat. Soap, bleach, fabric softener.

Aren't you a cutie-pie, Helene.

His face said as much.

"I'll pick some up. You okay with what's in the machines, or would you like me to get you something as well? My treat."

Helene liked a cappuccino. A double shot of espresso. Liked it from the barista at the Coop Market coffee bar.

"Passed it on my way here. See what I can do."

And he did. He returned. She thanked him for her beverage. Gave him money.

"I said it was my treat."

"We are not dating, you and me. Though, if you are planning a heist..."

Michael. Nonplussed. "I thought I erased my history."

"And I erased it from my server. About this heist of yours, I will give you a pillowcase for my share of the loot."

Helene turned back to her weaving.

Michael, back to the internet. Back to work. Cevik provided the dart; Michael wasn't sure he'd even thrown it at a wall. He needed to contact Lynn. Without contact.

Design a signal only Lynn will know. A code inside it she can decipher without a key.

He didn't doubt she would. He would need her to. He had nothing. A private Swiss bank. Assets—at least as recently as 2010—of 2.2 billion dollars. Millions in change. Right in the Goldilocks of all the banks in Switzerland—not too hot, not too cold, too rich, too poor, just right in the don't-look-at-me middle.

Same for President/CEO Antonio Abbatantuono—the silver-haired banker he biometrically identified when first arrived in Geneva. Before he ditched the device.

"Helene?"

"Yes, Mr. Without-a-name American Joe."

"Amazing coincidence. It is Joe. You know anything about Antonio Abbatantuono? Runs that bank I'm thinking of robbing."

Without looking into the mirror. "He's my husband."

"*Sans autres.* And have you ever met?"

She remained bent over her work, but not so much Michael couldn't see that pixieish grin of hers. She shook her head, judging him as if he were the fool to play into her sarcasm. She said nothing more. Michael kept digging at Pell & Glatisant. Like digging a hole in the air. And his mind wandered.

A carousel. Knights' horses. A unicorn. A panther. A wild boar. And one of those sled-shaped seats for the smallest of children to ride side-by-side with a parent.

A sleigh in the shape of a leopard.

The head of a snake.
Lion haunches.
The feet of a stag.
Lynn in her stroller. A red balloon. Jousting knights.
Kalaydoskop kisses his mother.

♛ ♛ ♛

"Wake up."

A whisper. Right in his ear. Tender.

Gwen?

"You can heal in your room. I am closed now."

Michael rolled his neck. Met Helene's eyes. She was still close. The gray iris encircled by a faded purple limbal ring. Beautiful eyes. This close, young and ageless.

"You wasted your computer time. I provide no refunds."

"Big deal. I'm robbing a bank."

"No, you're not. I do think I know what you *are* doing. We can discuss it over dinner."

"Now who is trying to date whom?"

She gave Michael a patient smile. She offered him her hand. He felt strange.

If I take that hand—Shit. If I touch her, accept human connection—I'm going to fall apart.

Helene pretended she didn't see him swallow the lump in his throat. Her hand hovered.

"If it's all the same, I'd rather not go out. Tonight. Probably not at all, while I'm here."

"I'm inviting you to dinner with me. Upstairs. Where I can also help you treat what hurts you. Don't make a pass or what hurts you will be me."

♕ ♕ ♕

Helene Favre occupied a split-level apartment above her shop. Filled with enough potted palms to fill a *Thief of Baghdad* movie set. Doorways hung with beads. Silks. Lots of warm woods and all of them carved, Art nouveau and faintly mystical. The aroma of chicken cassoulet with sausage and Swiss chard filled her chambers and, soon, filled Michael's stomach to nourish him body and soul and all he could say was...

"This tastes amazing. When did you find time to whip this up? While I was sleeping?"

"Four days ago. Possibly when you were getting beaten up? So, *remettre l'église au milieu du village.*"

"Helene, I don't speak French."

"'Let us put the church back at the center of the village,' no?"

"And not even English, apparently."

"Come-come. At first, I thought it might be your wife."

"I'm not married."

God. I'm not. Gwen—what have we done?

"The tan line and groove around your fingers speaks its own language as well."

"Well. Yeah. We just got divorced."

"This is difficult for you... So, it is not what I ultimately *didn't* suspect. Monsieur Antonio Abbatantuono is able—financial power, social position, political clout—able to keep himself off the internet and mostly out of the press, but he is unable to keep his hands off beautiful women. Media never acknowledges it. They protect him. That protects our banking. But he is notorious for poaching tourists' wives. He is a troublesome man with a strong libido. He likes foreign women, and he does this for sport."

"And husbands and boyfriends get hurt."

"Hurt and paid."

"Aha. My cash."

"Your cash. Now we're both smart."

"But wrong."

They were enjoying each other immensely and were in sync. It wasn't a surprise that they both said, *sans autres* at the same time. Obviously. The surprise for Michael came next. He watched his hostess excuse herself from the table and take a folded sheet of printer paper from her purse.

She stood before him, holding the page to her thin chest. She said, "His wife has finally had enough of him. She has filed for divorce over his latest fling who isn't going home."

"Is that the article I missed? Protects him, protects banking, *sans autres.*"

"Obviously, but no." She placed it on the table before him. "This comes from our local newspaper. Their archives are not in English translation and are not easily found. Open it."

Michael did.

Helene said, "You complimented me on how well I aged. This is Monsieur Abbatantuono. A boisterous celebration luncheon; his bank's founding day. You can see how handsome a fox he has always been."

Michael studied the man she pointed out. "But he didn't age nearly as well as you—though you have made some interesting hair and make-up changes."

Michael followed her finger as it traced to an exuberant young woman. Champagne flute, one hand. Ceremonial pen, the other, like Audrey Hepburn's cigarette holder in *Breakfast at Tiffany's*. Doris Kingston smiled at Michael from out of the past.

Wednesday, July Seventh

1.

T HE FOG CLEARED. HER mind engaged. Terror seized Lynn with the realization that her air intake regulated through the bottom of her throat. A nasogastric tube filled her right nostril. Bore into her innards. Reflex drove her body upward, hands upward to rip the feeding tube from her nose. Her heels pounded the foot of her bed, but restraints allowed her the freedom of movement to do nothing else.

Airport. Scissors. Throat.

Blood. Michael. Dead not-Michael.

She racked her gaze. Hospital bed. Vital monitors. NG feed. IV pumps—

Rusty Aiken, night, guilt, ghost.

—and a doctor, beneath the television monitor. Image: a mossy waterfall tinkling in time to cocktail lounge Mozart. The doctor turned from a communications whiteboard, where he's written pharmaceutical notations. Turned at the sound of her feet.

"Ms. Kingston. Perfect timing. Welcome back from outer space, eh? This will calm you the most: your tracheostomy is absolutely and one hundred percent temporary."

Lynn tried to speak. Croaked. Clenched at the pain.

"Everyone tries. Now you know to try not to. We've equipped your tracheostomy tube with a PMV—that's a Passy-Muir Valve—it's a speaking valve you will use before we remove your tube. However—Oh—"

He was beside her now. Lynn relaxed. Chest heaved. Tube doing its work as she deep breathed her way out of the pain.

"I'm Dr. Goldfarb." A gentle handshake. "I'm your Attending Physician—means I'm the surgeon who treated your wound. That was three nights ago." He tracked her eyes to the wall clock. 4:18. "We're early-early morning on the seventh."

Lynn blinked. Unbidden, her eyes flooded.

"I thought you might regain consciousness this morning. I lingered after my shift. Wanted to be here for you. You must have an angel, because you were extraordinarily lucky...and you got me and I'm extraordinarily very-very, *very* good."

She gave him a wan smile.

"When the residents come around, they're going to bore you with all the details. They will provide you with a tablet device to communicate with, but all you really need to know—because this takes you from your present condition to throat closed and out of here—is that your assailant nicked your vocal cords on both sides. They're going to heal; you will fully recover your speech, but you can imagine the swelling. The passage of air across them, using them at all, will only exacerbate, maybe even inhibit, your best recovery. You shouldn't be feeling any pain, but you should feel the thickness of the swelling."

Lynn probed her injury with her mind.

A softball stuck in my throat. What will I do without a voice—? He said you'll get it back. I'll get it back. I'm alive. I will be fine.

Feeling great, actually. Ha!

Her own sarcasm didn't amuse her. More eye-flood. Blinked again.

Thank you so much, Dr. Goldfarb.

Her fingers twitched for his. He linked them to his own.

Thank you.

He nodded, *yes.* He understood. Soon she slept.

👑👑👑

NURSES WITH "Aren't these lovely, dear," flowers. Balloons noosed to teddy bears; reading: "'Get well, Aunt Linny! We miss you! Love, Paige, Charlotte, and Leigh?' Your nieces?"

Two, anyway.

Torso unstrapped. Arms freed. "We'll have to redo them when you fall asleep. It's a natural impulse. Most people try to remove the equipment while they are unconscious. Until you get used to it."

The residents. In like conventioneers, going booth to booth taking notes. One beclowned herself, offering Lynn a fancy folder brochure for the hospital. Their mother hen, true to Dr. Goldfarb's prediction, had a lot to say. All very technical, all very well-reasoned, all very post-operative/acute-care cute-as-a-button Dr. Shirakawa—Harajuku girl transplant—who twittered and acted like this should be the happiest day of Lynn's life.

It is, you ungrateful sourpuss.

Like back in school; Lynn tuned them all out until they got to the tablet. "Tap here on the home screen. It opens the program with a cursor ready to go. I get it instantly on mine. Better than talking. No confusion."

Lynn: *Did I have visitors while I was out?*

A resident showed Dr. Shirakawa the question on the paired tablet.

Dr. Shirakawa: *Your father, and your brother.*

Lynn: *You can answer me out loud.*

"Of course. Just wanted to get you comfortable with the interface." Consulted another resident's clipboard. "Your brother, Mr. Hal Kingston, came yesterday. But your father arrived while you were in surgery. He stayed with you in the post-op recovery until you moved to this room. Apparently, he didn't sign out."

Lynn: *Vanished. He does that. Does this get me internet access?*

"Ms. Kingston. Yes, it does. What you need, though, is rest."

Lynn: *Night-night.*

She put the tablet aside. Shut her eyes. Presently, a nurse leaned in to strap her down.

♛ ♛ ♛

NOW SHE HURT. Now she woke. Whatever they were giving her it was time for more. Wasn't two minutes, and some nurse she'd not seen before came in. Freed her arms.

Lynn: *Thanks.*

Ding. The tablet on the countertop. A glance. "No worries." He went about his business, chatting aimlessly.

Lynn: *Were you here when any of my family visited?*

Read. Responded, "I think Janella might've been. She's around here, somewhere. I'll find her."

He did. Janella: "Yes. I was here, Ms. Kingston. Set you up in this bed myself."

Lynn mustered a faint smile of appreciation.

"Rotating shifts starting today. You'll have me the next two mornings. Wish it could be more, but if I don't take my vacation week, I lose the days."

She noticed Lynn's perplexed expression.

"Oh. Right. You wanted to know about visitors."

Lynn typed: *My father sat with me?*

"Most of the first night."

Lynn: *You remember what kind of hair he had?*

Janella laughed. "Trick question. His head's smooth as a baby's bottom."

Lynn scowled. Typed. *"Was there another man? At night. Curly hair. Gray with some brown. In his sixties."*

"No. No one else came any night I'm aware of." She narrowed her eyes. "You see someone?"

Lynn tried to nod. Hurt.

"You came in under police protection. They got removed, though. You're some kind of Fed, but don't worry, I know better than to ask."

She noticed Lynn's puzzlement. Her concern. "Ms. Kingston. This, what we give you, can make for hallucinations. Folks see people—other things—"

Grip my hand as hard as you can... Grip my voice...listen.

"Talk to 'em—at least, think they do. Now this isn't medical, but it's what I tell all my patients. You get those sorts of visitors: you force yourself to laugh." Tapped the side of her head. "In here. Laugh right in their faces. Poof! They're usually gone and don't come back."

Gladys. Sent. All you need to know. Gladys. Sent.

Whir. The narcotic drip cycled. Janella checked it. Checked every read-out. Straightened blankets. Soothed. "That's gonna knock you out a bit."

Gladys. Nathan Muir's former secretary.

"But I'm not too busy. You're not fidgety. Let's see if we can leave your arms free. Here. I'll tuck them under your blanket. Like so..."

Gladys Jlassi.

"...I'll keep peeking in. You're a fighter. You'll be just fine."

Rusty Aiken's caretaker for his daughter. Jessie. Over the years, Gladys sends invitations. Emails. I ignore but don't delete. I missed something?

Lynn zonked out.

❦❦❦

Awake. Eyeline: telephone.

Call him.

Reaching. Lifting the receiver. Voice test. "Heeh-ooh." Rasping, tear-bringing, burning pain. Sank back into her pillow. Wiped eyes. Listened to the strange hiss of her trach tube. Watched her heart rate spike. Willed/waited for it to decrease.

Do better. "Gladys sent." Emails.

Maybe he *was* a hallucination.

Not true.

Lynn finger-fumbled for her tablet. Navigated to her personal email. Navigated to the *Inbox. Search* bar. Input: *Gladys Jlassi.* Autocomplete provided the address. *Click.* Six email invitations to Jessie Aiken events:

Subject: Help Us Celebrate: Jessie's High School Graduation – May 2008

Subject: Help Us Celebrate: Jessie Turns 18! – July 2008

Subject: Help Us Celebrate: Jessie Turns 19! – July 2009

Opened/ignored. Innocuous invites.

Subject: Help Us Celebrate: Jessie Turns 20! – July 2010

Opened—the year Rusty retired. Lynn brought up Jessie's birthday. Moment of weakness; afraid to lose him—not that he was ever hers to lose. Day Aiken delivered Muir's desk to her office. He didn't mention any party. She thought better of it. All of it. Nina, his wife; their happiness. Opened/Ignored.

Subject: Help Us Celebrate: Jessie Turns 21! – July 2011

Unopened/ignored. Lynn opened it now. Same heading. A date. A time. An address: Nina's U Street Corridor three-level railroad house. A beaming photo of their Russian daughter. Lynn deleted it. Somehow hated herself.

That was it. And then, *Ding!* That wasn't "it" at all. New email in her inbox.

What d'ya know?

From Gladys Jlassi. *Subject: Help Us Celebrate: Jessie Turns 22!* Lynn opened the email. Not an invite. None of the earlier info. No photo. Only this: *One word. Not two.*

Lynn deleted the message.

2.

*T*HE SORRY STATE OF *American jury prudence. That's what this is.*

Thirty minutes kept waiting. Less than that when she got in with her attorney. The *Voted Best Family Law Practice in the Maryland Tri-State*. Erika Newhoff. A-number-one idiot. The ridiculousness. Simply trying to fix a simple error of judgment.

Isn't the law supposed to fix things that are wrong? Legal mistakes rectified? Like a man and wife want to cancel a divorce: move national statistics in the right direction. For once.

"You're well within the thirty-day period for a reversal to a final divorce decree allowed by Maryland law."

"Great. Let's do it."

"Mr. Kingston is in agreement?"

"Would I be here if he wasn't?"

"I can schedule a hearing for both of you before a judge. I will contact his lawyer."

"His lawyer's the guy who talked him *into* the divorce."

Erika Newhoff owl-eyed her.

"Gwen—you filed for divorce. Our offices served your ex-husband."

"I don't need details on facts I already know. And dispute. Michael is overseas anyway and won't be home within thirty days. He's in government service. The kind you, me, the judge aren't permitted to talk about. So I am sure there's a way around that."

"I'm not." Drummed her pen on her legal pad. "I supposed were he able to give an affidavit at whatever official offices he serves. Have it notarized..."

"Oh, my God. This can't be the first time. *In history*. This has happened."

"Yes. It could be. And he would have to be available for examination—albeit in writing—by the judge."

Gwen stood. Puffed out her ample chest. "Erika, do me the favor of printing out the whatever-document/form number-number-dash-letter bullshit we need to both sign, me n'Michael, to get this ball rolling. I will take it from there."

Erika Newhoff smiled, pleasant as a scorpion. Joined her client on her feet. "Of course, Gwen." Asked her to wait in the firm's lobby for her legal secretary to bring it out to her.

Waited twenty more minutes to be told it wasn't readily available, but they would be happy to email it no later than tomorrow.

Paige is right. "Family" ought to be stricken out of "Family Law" when all I'm doing is trying to make mine whole. They should bend over backwards for a victory for family sanctity like this.

Now who can I get to notarize Michael's signature if I do it?

Nelson Fair. Easy as done. Seeing him for lunch and a walk-through.

Gwen checked her Cartier. She had Nelson at 1 p.m. Bitch Newhoff had kept her waiting on her androgenous assistant until 11:50 a.m. She still had to swing by the July Fourth house—

Four offers and, ca-ching, closed. Way to go, babe.

—and resolve the missing Persian hallway runner.

We just sold your fucking house and you're gonna steal my rug? Crooks everywhere. My God.

She thumbed the steering wheel button. "Dial Nelson Fair," she commanded the Volvo, which responded, *"Dialing Nelson Fair,"* and Gwen, for the thousandth time, reminded herself she'd test out the hands-free system on her next car—

Finally, Michael's objections out of the way, I'll get the Mercedes this career requires.

—and make sure it's a car that doesn't sound like it's scolding her.

Nelson answered. She delivered the bad news. Lunch wasn't in the cards; Gwen would meet him at the new listing and maybe they'd "eat in" there.

"Gwen, I have been waiting for you to ask."

♔ ♔ ♔

INFIDELITY WASN'T THE CAUSE of Gwen's and Michael's divorce. She knew Michael had never been with another woman; Michael loved Gwen one hundred percent, body, mind, and spirit. Likewise—and she consulted the dictionary to check off the morality of it all—the Latin root for the word, *infidelis*, meant *unfaithful, treacherous, not to be trusted*; Gwen had erred to the side of faithfulness to her family and to her love for Michael; he knew he could trust her with everything that was important. She would *never* leave him for, fall in love with, or even crush on another man. She was his mate; he was hers, and that was their honor, duty, and country for life.

Even if they couldn't remain married any longer.

Even if Michael is dead.

I've made this family run. He knows/knew that. Much longer than was healthy. A lot longer than anyone else would have lasted.

Different career goals. I finally made him understand.

Objective differences in how we would finance our family's lifestyle and where and with whom we would spend our money and our time.

Not all over the armpit of the world.

Not all the time Silas forever-in-our-shit.

Gwen needed to escape the madness.

And now, those differences—the crux, the money of it all—are in jeopardy if we remain divorced and Michael, you're gone. I know you. I loved you. You want us to have the money entitled to us as a family.

All this was going through her mind as she rolled off Nelson Fair and planted the first seeds of getting him to notarize the statement that she was already coming up with, that she would affix Michael's signature.

He stared off, thinking about it. She secretly checked her Cartier.

God dammit, this guy wasting my time trying to get me off. As if. Late for the girls, and those idiot school pickup line volunteers with their judgmental looks.

The girls get it. Their mom works for a living.

GWEN'S PENCHANT for infidelity was not the cause of her divorce from Michael Kingston. That was a secret. A weird vice she liked to do at other people's homes, where she staged properties for sale. A weird gag—not all too unusual—practiced by more realtors and design-ers than most people could ever imagine. There was even a term for it in the industry. "Christening for mar-ket," and, by the way, three of the six men she'd gotten off with were in committed gay relationships. It was just a thing; like Tony said, "You can't have passion for a home until you've had passion in a home."

Someone always gets fucked in a real estate deal; might as well be me.

Not to say what she'd hinted to Lynn/Melody—the CIA-crazy-train—had nothing to do with it. Michael was a good father and a good provider and a tender, loving husband. Something she was now going to make sure everyone knew if she hoped to quash the judgment. The fact of the matter, she could feel it in her bones: Michael had lived way out on the edge, *not* saving the world, and now he'd stumbled off and was dead for it. If divorced before *that* event, she would be excluded from all benefits the CIA paid plenty to widows.

Michael used to be fun. And funny. They did fun things. He made her laugh. He made everyone laugh. He just stopped being all that—fun, funny, a good time had by all. Gwen was bored. It didn't help that no one saw it but her. The girls, especially. They didn't even care that he wasn't around like other dads. He had them fooled—especially Paige, who was old enough to know better—that he was still a riot. But how was Gwen supposed to have fun doing kid stuff? Where was the going out all night and blowing up on the dance floor? In Ankara, where were the embassy parties, the yachts, the secret agent highlife? What a waste of two years. Six months home. Six months of "date night" and a babysitter and the next morning—playing dollhouse with the girls, setting everything up, putting the plastic family all in their fake plastic places. Fake plastic furniture matched just right to fake plastic smiles.

Then you go and want all of us back to Ankara? You gotta be shitting me.

Oh, the other thing they called it was "Nailing a new listing." And honestly, out of the six, three were straight—but they were married and that made them one-offs and not a risk to her married life, and the other three were gay and just in it for fun. And to tell the truth, the pleasure she drew from it wasn't the physical part. Fucking *did* make her closer to the work at hand, made her more creative, really opened her up to her deepest artistic capabilities. Afterward, lying in someone else's bed, staring at their bedroom, showering in the showers, barefooting their rugs, their floors, their carpets, washed her with real design vision.

It's naughty. Okay, fine. I'm a bad girl. Dirty girl. That's only because Michael wasn't the bad boy he'd sold himself to me. The bad boy the black gold ring promised. A spy—aren't they supposed to be the ultimate bad boys? Wasn't James Bond the ultimate "bad boy?" Fiction, sure. But the author, whatisname-British, Michael said he'd been an actual spy, so he must have been writing from some kind of experience.

Not mine.

The deeper Michael got into his career, the more he faded into the background of every other facet of his life. If he wouldn't give her the Bond Girl experience, she'd get it herself. (And it really was five times, because two of her gay paramours came as a package deal.)

Just once—in Ankara the first time—if he couldn't deliver on the Ian Fleming (that's the cheerio's name) experience, if he'd at least given them the Maria von Trapp in the graveyard trip, maybe it wouldn't have come to this.

"What a boring life you've given me."

"Honey, I'm supposed to be boring."

"Well, go to the front of the line."

♔ ♔ ♔

UNBELIEVABLE. Late enough to swoop right in—not blocking anyone, holding anyone up, and they still give me shit eyes when they *are the ones who sent the girls up to Enrichment.*

Scowl at me. Here's a big, juicy smile for you, Mrs. Culpepper, sitting your fat ass on your crossing guard beach chair. (Nicey-nice, Gwen.)

Gwen waved her phone. Finger-pointed. Mouthed, *I texted.*

"Mrs. Kingston?" Knuckles on the window.

Clive Lancer. Ah-ha-ha.

Gwen activated her window. Raised her Persols. "Mr. Lancer. Tell me you're interviewing for a teaching position. Or any position."

Clive grinned. Ignored the innuendo.

"I wanted to surprise Paige. Take her to coffee in the old town. Look around at the history. If that's okay?"

"A walk around the square. Paige likes the Turtle Mud at the ice cream shop." She twisted her spine, stretching her shoulders back. "These leather seats are not as comfortable as they look. Especially when these old moms make you wait." Showed off her breasts.

"That would be okay?" Impervious.

"Here they come now. Ask her yourself." She lowered her glasses. Hot and cold running Gwen; she faced her windshield.

"Clive!" Paige said. Rushed over. Stopped short of throwing arms around him.

He stepped them away from Gwen's window. Up it shot.

"I was waiting for you. Wanted to see if you wanted to get a coffee. You could show me the Historic Town Center—" last three words: intentional nerd voice.

Paige gazed at him. Delighted. Said: "I thought you only drank tea."

"Shut up. Let's go." Another knock on Gwen's window. She returned his wave with the same smile she'd given Mrs. Culpepper.

"Hi, Clive!"

"Hello, girls."

Leigh: "Are you coming to Paige's birthday? Please-say-yes."

Paige: "We'll see."

3.

S ILAS HAD BEEN SERIOUS with Melody when she'd moved into the manor house—that she make sure to lock all the doors to prevent thieves. Each night, however, she always left one side door open. Her way of saying, he supposed, "This will always be your home." Tonight, after his three-day absence, Melody left the front door unlocked. Silas entered his generational home thinking—

Even with Hal fully armed, fully capable, the women and children are too much to risk with those who might come in the night. Especially with Gwen and the girls on the porch.

Silas smirked as he made his way to the center hall.

Gwen begged off staying. Silas challenged her on her love for Michael. She wanted a room. Told her to ask Melody—knowing her pride would prevent her. He rubbed it in.

"When they get the dog, it will want to be on the porch."

"I thought you said outside dog."

"Wrong as usual. A puppy needs to be indoors so Melody can hear it if it cries at night."

He'd have to do something about Gwen. About the divorce she thought he knew nothing about.

In darkness, he crept to the main stairway landing, seeking invisibility from Hal and his family upstairs, Gwen and the girls encamped on the east porch (until such a time as Michael's situation resolved). He peered upward. Into his dead wife's face bathed in moonlight, Doris washed in memories.

They say, if you stare at a portrait of someone you know, someone you love, you can read in their expression what they were thinking/feeling in the moment captured; in their eyes, you will see what quality of their humanity was/is/will-always-be their soul's illumination. In viewing the portrait of a stranger, the canvas invites you to know its subject by the reverse process of matching their expression to times/places/feeling of your own experience; of guiding off their eye light to the inner light within yourself. Silas knew this, but also knew, and better than most, that all art is a false reality. Deception at its most lovely. Seductive. A representation of a representation (since each human is only a representation of the true/pure form of what it is to take the form God made human). But this artist had been a genius. His portrait of Doris had transcended its own humanity.

Love and betrayal. Faith and humiliation. Unrelenting sin and unforgiven forgiveness.

Love is not binary; all good or all bad, all happy or all sad. Truly experienced, it is not scalable; it can be both simultaneously repugnantly annoying and embracingly euphoric. Love, like art, was a representation of the eternal form of God.

Doris was all these things. Doris lived them. Doris was dead.

Silas lived none of these things because—fear. Because danger. But in form, he too was all these things, because he was less alive than the painting that joined the two of them, with the artist and the third man, the man who was that fire in Doris's eye, eyes Silas commissioned this portrait to capture, and the fire Doris brought them, that helped kill her. That she would always blaze within. Her voice entered him:

I blazed in your eyes and never allowed you to see my tears. Because those tears were God's prayers to me.

GOD'S PRAYERS were also groans and grunts. The soul-howl, not from the head or the heart, but the gut—where you intrinsically know. The sound, loud and miserable, emanated from Silas as he hacked and thrashed with the machete out in the night, out deep beyond the old tobacco fields.

The agricultural portion of Foxtail Farm is laid out as a squared clock. Or compass. Or a cross. Four sectors of fields—the top and bottom of the vertical, the left and right of the horizontal—around a central hub that served as a crossroads. The four trapezoidal quadrants between the longitudinal and latitudinal axes provided for the buildings. Tool sheds. Stables. Mill. Air curing. Flue curing. Sorting and bundling. Traces and even structures—like the drying sheds and the smithy remains. Stone fertilizer and ash cribs.

The slave quarters, kitchen, latrines—the furthest section south. All of that was gone. Razed during the Civil War. Rebuilt for sharecropper farmers who'd worked the plantation until 1916, when Foxtail Farm volunteered a company for General Pershing's Punitive Expedition into Mexico to hunt down Pancho Villa. While their men were gone, Silas Kingston IV evicted their families from the property. This area of Foxtail Farm is now an overgrown wood. Its shameful history, hidden by bramble.

Buried furthest back was an even worse bit of horror. A plot of land known during the earliest years of slavery in the colony as "Turkey's Swan Song." Grave markers long rotted away, those with stones—the stones broken, scattered, or thrown from the bluffs to the river below.

Bitter land and bitterly overgrown.

Buried by foliage and left to remain, there was, deep inside, a simple stone bench.

The Silvanus Bench.

A seat from which the first patriarch oversaw his slave hunter dig graves and bury what he claimed. The place where each Silas Kingston patriarch went to contemplate their bloodline sins. The blood on their forefather's hands. Or hatched the plans that—spilled blood be damned—would continue the Kingston line and Foxtail Farm. Only the current patriarch sat here. No one else. Forbidden Silas as a child, he forbade it to his children. The children of his own three children were unaware of its existence.

Silas sat here the first three years after his return from Moscow. Nights he couldn't stand to make love to his wife. He returned during the portrait sessions between

Doris and the artist Boone, but now it huddled in bracken, crowned by thorns, invisible to all but Silas and God. But like God, he knew it; he saw it, unseen, and he hacked his way to his bench with a machete oiled with his misery.

Kolya had said, with Michael involved and Lynn, he could not guarantee the original condition of their long-standing agreement. That was the circumference of how the kaleidoscope now turned. For all of them.

Silas hacked and chopped and shredded his palms, fingers, pulling, snapping, and breaking branches like little necks. His nose and mouth and his eyes filled with the stink, the taste, and the sting of ash from hundreds of years of wood burned in the flue-curing of tobacco, tilled back into the soil as fertilizer.

♛ ♛ ♛

TULA. A plate of mushrooms gone cold. Mushroom cloud of the telephone in his fist. And just like that your life, as you know it, planned it, prayed it, is over.

"You were her friend. She's practically a girl." Silas.

"For someone trusted so well by your government in a position so important. They've put so much faith in you...and you put faith in me?" He tsk-tsk'd his tongue.

"I put my highest faith in my wife."

"No justice in that—our line of work or any other, I think."

"Love is its own justice."

"Should be its own justice, mmm? But, sadly, no. It is not. The least of justice lies is in love. But we'll save

that for another day. Perhaps the American cancer gets excised, and the world finds itself at peace. You are running out of time. Their lives for yours."

Silas sat on the carved-stone Silvanus Bench. Head heavy in his hands. Fire in his eyes so stuffed by ash he could not cry and because he could not cry, he was as dead and unreal to God as the bones of the runaways Turkey John Swann had captured who had vanished in this soil of Foxtail Farm. Beneath the earth beneath his feet.

When Doris sat for her birthday portrait, the expression Boone captured was her love of Silas as one side of a two-sided coin. Kolya was on the other side. The tragedy of the full cup of life.

Children off limits. Kolya/Kaladoskop agreed.

Trained to find people's vulnerabilities. What are their motivations? Is it flattery or vanity or revenge? Do they hate their job, their boss? Adventure-fantasy, Midas Greed, desire for live-like-the-other-half creature comforts? Silas Kingston's was family. A promise now broken.

Head, heart, gut. A full body/soul cringe. An *ugh* made him want to spit every time he thought of it, which for thirty years was hundreds of times. Every. Single. Day.

Thursday, July Eighth

1.

A *JOUSTING KNIGHT. BLUE tunic over rust-speckled armor. The point of a lance strikes his breast. Horses pass. The armored dummy clangs against his horse's croup.*

"Lynn…"

Horses crank round. Blue knight cranks up. Raised from robot dead.

"It's me." The voice belonged to a hand. The hand stroked her hair. Strong. Warm. Male. Tender.

Rusty…

"Can you hear me, Lynn? Can you wake up a minute?"

Lynn's eyelids pulled apart. She focused on Deputy Director for Operations Gary Gravin.

More real than Aiken. A better knight for me. Equally unavailable.

She matched his smile. Bathed in its warmth for a moment while her mind took stock.

Same bed. Same hospital. Another day. Same wound.

"Hi."

Only now did he remove his hand from her hair, trailing the back of it down her cheek. She grabbed it. Briefly. Just a squeeze before it passed out of range. Lynn elevated the bed.

"I hope you liked the flowers," he said.

Lynn nodded. He pointed to a chair. Lynn nodded. He pulled it beside her and sat. Their faces were level. Lynn nodded, *Go on...?*

He said, "The press has run with the story that the victim, who *wasn't* your brother, was a heroin courier with a shipment out of Afghanistan. Nothing close to the truth, but what do they say about not letting a good crisis go to waste? We bombed the shit out of several al Qaeda and Taliban sites in retaliation."

Lynn picked up her tablet. Indicated he pick up its twin from the sink counter. She typed: *Ring, jacket, cover passport. Those were my brother's.*

"They were. Though the 'Arthur Danford' passport is strange. Technical Services reports that it is a very good forgery of our original forgery issued to Michael. What's going on? You need to tell me everything you know."

Lynn stared.

"I'm on your side. I'm on Michael's side."

Lynn stared harder.

"He's your brother—I get the extra caution, I do, and I'm willing to give you latitude. Some. But that's got to go two ways. He's my officer. Serves my directorate. I don't for a minute believe he's caused any of this. He's the target. I want to protect him, but God dammit, Lynn—" eyes flashing hard, anger threatening to break through— "my directorate isn't a Kingston sandbox. You want my support, my respect, an official stamp rather than an oversight investigation that's going to lead to warrants—? You better write this up—every fact, every detail you've hidden from me. Every word of every off-the-record conversation you and Michael have had, then throw in every conjecture you've drawn, *followed by* every wild-ass guess you can make that puts some meat and muscle on the bones of this very rickety skeleton of an unsanctioned operation before it turns into a grim reaper cutting *off* heads." He drew a breath. "All of ours."

Lynn typed: *KALEIDOSCOPE.*

Gary gripped the pad two-handed. Looked ready to smack her head with it. Refrained. "Don't go there. I warned you. You better find something else."

Lynn typed: *The flowers are lovely.*

Gary readjusted in his seat. Simmered. The pain in Lynn's eyes wasn't physical. She reached out for him. He hesitated a fraction of a second before he gave her hand a squeeze. Her thoughts reeled.

He's got my back if I let him. He's smart. He knows it's personal. Let it go. Let him in.

He proved it adding his other hand, clasping hers with both of his. "Even if what happened to Michael abuts that program—which, repeat, repeat, repeat: we are to stay far away from—serious penalties, my friend; most serious—it's ours. We don't order hits on our own people. This—" he gestured at her wound. "This wasn't KALEIDOSCOPE. Cevik had something. Gave it to Michael, or at least debriefed on it. You know something you're not telling me, and it's pissing me off. You know how much I care for you. I can't help you, which means I can't help Michael if you cut me out."

Lynn nodded. For a moment, let the depth of her feelings for him gleam in her eyes. She slipped her hand free of his. Took up her tablet. Typed: *I hope it's only your name on the "get well" card.*

Acknowledged her words with irony. "It'll be my wife on the Senate committee with the sharpest..."

Lynn typed: *Scissors?*

"Yeah. Poor metaphor." An embarrassed snort. "Sorry about that."

Lynn typed: *There's nothing between us, Gary. But if it ever came down to taking the proverbial knife to protect you—the Agency—I'd do it.*

"Let's not let it get to that." He said, "They tell me you're healing beautifully. As soon as they can remove the tubes—you can eat and breathe for yourself—they'll release you. Possibly this weekend. At which time you'll be able to speak for yourself."

He put his tablet aside. Came to his feet.

"At that point, you'll help me help you. Write that report, Lynn. Take care."

Lynn typed: *Did they get the bitch who did this to me? Go a long way as motivation.*

Gary held back a moment. "She was some kind of pro. We're still looking."

As he rose to turn for the door, Lynn turned away. The meds made her emotional.

He stopped in the doorway. Recalled something else. "Drexler."

She question-marked him with her eyebrows.

"He informed me the Office of Security cleared your father a visit to headquarters."

Lynn's face filled with consternation.

"Drexler thinks Silas is coming to see me—about your brother, *my* officer." He shrugged. "Unlike you—hmm? I'll let you know whatever I find out."

☙❧❦

PAIGE SAID: "Aren't you the one who told me I text too much?"

Lynn typed: *Hilarious.* Typed: *Happy you're visiting. Is your mom coming up?*

"She doesn't know I'm here."

Lynn gave her wide-eyes.

"I never know where *she* is."

Typed: *Did Morgan bring you?*

Paige grabbed the paired tablet. She typed. *My new BF. Feel more comfortable texting that. Haha.* Said, "If you'd stayed longer on the Fourth, you'd have met him."

If I stayed longer, I wouldn't be here. Hahaha.

"I know I can't ask what happened. Or how. You all lie anyway. But I'm glad you're going to be okay. You are, right?"

Lynn spread her hands. Gave a look.

"Will you be able to talk? When they take all that out?"

Lynn tried to say yes. Came out, "Eheaeehh." Brittle. Harsh.

"Ow! Don't do that—that can't feel good. C'mon, Aunt Linny, you gotta let it heal."

Lynn squeezed back the pain from her eyes.

"You sure don't need to impress me. I *know* you're tough."

Tell me about your new BF.

"Here." She tapped her way to a photo on her smartphone. Paige and Clive. Town Square coffees. A cheers/grins selfie.

He's hot. He's OLDER. College?

Paige fidgeted. "He's English. Or British. Or whatever you say it. He was studying abroad—like, here. We met at the river."

Lynn's deceit radar pinged. *She's lying?*

"One of Morgan's bonfires. He decided he'd finish his summer in town."

Lynn typed. *Name?*

"Clive."

Typed: *Not much of a touristy place. Unless you're the attraction.* She watched her niece's reaction. Typed: *Blushing...*

They shared the moment, amused.

"I really like him. And he's really into me. And he's single, like, back home. And it's going really fast."

For the first time since waking up in her bed, Paige felt something like happiness.

Typed: *You want to know about "fast" and "too fast."*

Paige stared at her screen.

Lynn: *Why you're here, right?*

Paige didn't look up.

She's picked me. Instead of Gwen... Typed: *I can see you blushing again. Lolo?*

Paige typed. *Just one O.* Said, "L-o-l."

Lynn: *My take—You're seventeen and he's...NOT. And boys that age might want to go faster than maybe you're prepared for. Am I near the target?*

Paige said: "It's not that. Opposite." She typed: *"I want to and I'll be eighteen at one in the morning on Sunday, you know."* Then rushed past that. "You'll be able to come? I mean, Sunday night?"

Lynn nodded. Kind. Held her in a knowing look. Paige dropped her gaze. Lynn typed: *This last thing, though. You came here for SOMETHING from me. You got a good head on your shoulders, and I won't lecture you. But DON'T get pregnant.* Stern look—only half-joking. Typed: *No matter what you've heard: it only takes one time.*

Their eyes met. Uncomfortable. Just as Lynn could read lies, Paige could read truth in people. She gave her aunt a probing look like, *What are you telling me?*

Lynn ignored. Dangerous water. Typed: *Another thing. Don't ever, ever, ever do anything in your life—I'm talking beyond sex—anything that you know, going into it, that you know you'll feel guilty about later.*

"How do you predict that?"

Typed: *Because you learn—in what I do, your dad, your Uncle Hal, Papa—you learn to listen to your gut.*

"Yeah, right. That's kind of—I've never believed that whole 'Listen to your gut' thing."

Lynn raised a *wait* finger. Went at her tablet. *Every language, all around the globe—first world societies to Amazon tribes—they all have language that says "Trust/listen to your gut." Not one of them say, "Listen to your elbow." They all use GUT.*

"But isn't that just listening to your heart? Or your head? It's the 'gut' thing of it all. It's not like something I feel."

Lynn: *Feel harder. Don't mistake if for your head or your heart, when it comes from your gut. Because I've decided—in my unforgiving life—the gut's where God talks to you.*

Paige gazed at Lynn. Made the heart shape with her hands. Lynn caught the arrow of an idea.

Thought: *Gladyssent. One word, not two.*

"I better go. Clive's waiting. Thanks, Aunt Lynn."

Lynn waved her hand, *Sit. Wait.* Thought: *I've searched all day. I'm getting something wrong, but Paige...* Typed: *I need you to do one thing for me.*

"Okay..."

Typed: *I'm searching something online. I know it's there, but I've got the spelling totally wrong.*

"What can I do about that?"

Typed: *Your phone. The AI assistant. I can't use mine—duh. But when I do, it sometimes hears me wrong. Gives answers for something that sounds the same but spells/defines differently.*

Paige read Lynn's message. "Whatever—yeah, I get it. Easy-peasy." She hesitated. "Don't you have like five hundred people at work who do this sort of thing for a living?"

Lynn rolled her eyes. Typed: *It's personal. Something I remembered. It's for your dad. Sister-brother thing.*

Paige made a skeptical face.

Lynn typed: *Just do it. "Gladys. Sent." But as one word, not two.*

Paige laughed. At her.

Lynn human-emoji'd *What?!*

"You really don't know? A family thing? A you-and-dad thing? You *don't* remember? 'Gladys sent?'"

Angry eyes: Lynn. Delight: Paige. Raised her smartphone. "Search 'Glatisant.'"

The phone returned its answer. Paige turned around the screen.

Glatisant: the questing beast, Arthurian legend.

A series of images depicted a mythical creature. The head of a serpent. Body of a leopard. Powerful legs of a lion with the cloven hooves of a deer.

Thought/typed: *WTF?!*

"Aunt Linny! Come on! Grandma Doris's book. T.H. White *The Once and Future King*. It's the funny part. The dragon that King Pellinore is always questing after that falls in love with him."

A haunted look invaded Lynn's features. "Why would you say it, but not know it, *but* think of Dad?"

Lynn shook her head, bewildered.

"You're seriously weirding me out."

Typed: *These drugs. I've been having weird dreams. Kind of like that book. I just couldn't put it together/re-member.*

Typed: *How's your mom handling this new boyfriend of yours?*

"Not *boyfriend* to Mom. None of her business, any-ways."

Lynn: *Yet. Lololol*

Got a laugh. "Okay, '*yet*-anyways.' She's creeping on him. You know Mom. Like she's done with every guy I ever took an interest in. At school or who worked at the market or the pizza place. *Every* guy. Whenever dad's away."

Lynn couldn't hide her concern. Her judgement.

"She doesn't *do* anything. She's just..."

Lynn typed: *She sometimes runs hot.*

"Yeah. And luckily for everyone, they all run away. Otherwise, she's the coolest mom out there."

Typed: *She and Michael are great parents. You three girls wouldn't be so wonderful and the envy of everyone if they weren't... How are you doing with the whole thing with Dad?*

Ding! Paige checked her phone. "It's Clive. I gotta go. I'm fine. 'Nobody vanishes,' right?"

They shared a sad smile. Lynn raised her palm and gave a childish, cupped-hand bye-bye. Paige went back. Kissed her. Hurried out.

2.

*S*ILAS KISSES THE TOP *of Doris's coffin. Steps back to allow the mortuary crew to activate the winch. His wife and one true love is lowered into the stone tomb beneath the floor of the Foxtail Farm chapel.*

♕ ♕ ♕

"MELODY SAYS you want to discuss something with me?" Hal entered the chapel. His father kneeled in prayer over his mother's tomb.

Silas took his time to finish. Crossed himself. Stood. Gave Hal a discerning once-over.

Hal continued. "We're all curious where you rushed off to the other night."

"I visited your sister."

"You weren't there when we came." Hal leaned against the back of a pew. "You'd been back here and left again by the time the sun rose the next morning. Three days, Dad. At a time like this?"

"Don't interrogate me, Hal. You'll only step on a rake. Where I've been is trivial, and I won't tell you, anyway. I need action from you. We have a larger issue at hand only you can solve."

Hal waited for his father to elaborate. Silas busied himself, cutting open a fresh bouquet of red river lilies delivered and left on the stone baptismal font. Examined each lily for flaws, separating the bunch.

"How certain are you Michael survived your extraction?"

"One thousand percent."

"It only goes up to one hundred, and I should say, 'failed' extraction."

"I'll ignore the dig and repeat: I am certain Michael survived."

Silas placed the flowers into the waiting fluted silver stand. "Did you know Lynn went to Dulles to meet Michael?"

Hal cocked his head. "Had my suspicions."

"Did you know that the man traveling under Michael's passport Lynn and her team were there to collect was murdered?"

"Yeah. I heard the cover story running on the news. And I am sorry to hear it if he was Michael's asset. But, again, I'm not cleared for any of that and I'm not comfortable discussing whatever you know—however you know it."

Silas moved flower stalks, patiently making them perfect.

Hal added, "I would say that leads to the theory that Michael's adversaries are on the growing list that starts with me, includes Lynn and the Directorate of Operations, of those people certain Michael is alive."

Silas continued to concentrate on the arrangement, now only to get under Hal's skin.

"Okay, then." Hal pushed off the pew. "I want to get down to the beach with Gwen and the boys, so I'll throw you an easy target. Sounds to me—in your own crazy way—you'd prefer Michael dead."

"Obviously, I don't want my firstborn dead."

"So get to your 'why.' Why are we having a church meeting?"

"You need to change your official story. I must have you sworn on record that you saw him killed. Unequivocally."

"You know I can't do that."

"Save your duty, honor, country."

"That's Army's motto. I'm a Marine and straight up. I'll spell out the Marine Corps version in case you've forgotten. 'Never lie, never cheat or steal; abide by an uncompromising code of integrity; respect human dignity; and respect others.' That's what I've sworn my life to. Not going to change that and asking me is an insult and a waste of our time."

"Hear that, Doris? Nothing's going to make Hal happy until he can sacrifice his life for his country."

"Nope. Never said that. And Dad, *that*—mocking my mother—you won't get away with it twice."

"Yes. You're right. Thought you were Lynn for a minute—"

"Don't."

Silas leaned against the pew beside him. "Hal. Listen to me. Who would you sacrifice your life for first? Your country? Or your family?"

"I won't answer that."

"The only reason you defend your country is to protect your family. I would say you have a commitment far stronger to the protection of your family than to your country."

"You're an asshole. You really are. How does changing my story—committing a crime by giving my name to a blatant lie—protect my family?"

"They—whomever they were at Dulles—they think Michael's alive. You can help make it so they don't."

"Just to get this straight. I'm not doing this to protect my family, but Michael's? Don't think he'd ask that of me. Sorry."

"You're a Kingston. This is your whole family. And here's another thing you don't know—your sister-in-law, Gwen, divorced Michael shortly before he took off on his walkabout."

"What?"

"She's been scheming to take his money and my grandchildren—your nieces—since he re-posted. I can't believe I'm the only one around here smart enough to see through her pathetic schemes."

Hal took it like the hammer blow Silas intended. Pulled himself around the pew to sit. To look at the cross. To give his father his back.

"But if Michael's divorced—she gets nothing."

"Your official statement that he's alive allows Gwen to keep collecting his paycheck until he redesignates their direct deposit. Which Michael is in no position to do. I know what you believe you might have seen—what we all believe—but unless you saw him fully and completely escape, and we both know that certainty is impossible..."

"That certainty cuts both ways."

Silas squeezed his shoulder. "Don't put your US Marine Corps ahead of protecting those three young women from what undoubtedly would be a horrible, horrible future, adrift on the deck of the shipwreck with a loose cannon—and I use loose in all its forms—that's their mother's life."

"You're asking me to do something that will force me to resign." He glanced back at his father's face, looking for... Love? Trust? Honesty?

Quiet rage. "I am asking you to do what Michael cannot to save his children. Honestly, are you that selfish?"

"This is bullshit. She'll still get his death benefit."

"No. She won't. Michael 'dead' stops Gwen from collecting ongoing salary under Spousal Pay Entitlement 3403, while divorce locks her out of his CIA death benefits. I become trustee for Michael's benefits. As long as I have the money for those girls, Gwen won't take them anywhere."

Hal defined himself in pure and simple terms: selflessness—he glanced again at the cross—the purest term of all. He wilted into his pew.

Silas patted his shoulder and left him to his mother's bones and God.

♕ ♕ ♕

THE TIDE STROKED the mermaids' green hair, rhythmic hands curling over them, mantling their slick cypress shoulders with white, bubbling trails. The furnace of summer blasted high at Foxtail Farm immediately after July 4th, as though the explosives of that night had rent an atmospheric tear that ran straight to the sun. Melody was thankful—along with everything else this Kingston life had brought her—for the beach. Its seclusion, its safety for the children, its timelessness. Even its history; strange and twisted like her own. Try as she might, she could not rid herself of her conversation with Jack. The other day on the stairs. The coming doom reminded her. Sworn to initiate, she'd vowed to deny.

She watched her twin boys frolicking. She couldn't deny the emergence of their grandfather's features in their faces. How, in bliss, it was a face handsome and free of the devil—a classic American face with a twinkle in the eye that, allowed to grow true into adulthood, would glow with nobility. Would become an honest face that men and women would gladly hold before them and follow with their hearts.

It was not Silas's face Melody saw on her sons. It was the face her father had been born with—the face the man lost to the devil.

Melody felt the skin on her feet burning. She smeared them with sunscreen. She thought, *These feet I got from my mother.*

♛ ♛ ♛

A MAN'S white tube sock. Tip stuck beneath the tubular, aluminum leg of the second-hand kitchen table. Mama's foot pulled from the sock in falling. She lies backwards from the table.

I can't see the rest of her. Squatting, my bottom touching the floor, my arms around my shins, my face buried in my knees. My teeth bite the skin and I taste my blood.

The sole of Mama's foot is the color of the top of my foot.

The top of her foot is the color of my eyes.

Except for the blood. Mama's blood. Until turpentine washes it clean. I cannot move. I stare as the turpentine evaporates on her black foot, momentarily coating it white. More spirits of turpentine splash over it. Over the floor from over the table and the chair she pulled down, and I know, it spills all over her body, torn dress revealed. Naked as the day she was born.

Naked as I was born, and she first held and first loved me.

I cannot see her. Know—huddled and shaking and biting, too afraid to make actual tears—that I will never see her again.

"Mama?"

"You know she hears only angels now. Be a good girl, Mel. Get your mother's sewing basket. Get her new-made dresses, her patterns, and her portable machine you're learning on, and get out to the car."

The smell of the gun. Full and sharp and imagined everlasting just five minutes ago, the smell of the gun overwhelmed by the vile stench of Daddy's spirits. "I can't do all that in one trip."

"Then you'll hurry your fanny and make two because this hellhouse is gonna burn."

My eyes say goodbye to Mama's foot.

My foot grows into her foot. Walking back roads, railroad tracks, walking sides of highways and city-rough side streets with my daddy. Working the sewing machine pedal. I learn the measure of his plan. I cut my way to Smyrna, stitch my way here where Daddy patterned his ruin and intends to ruin those who pinned it to him.

♔ ♔ ♔

FIRST PAGE Search Results, first return: Glatisant – The Questing Beast.

   Green head of a snake.
   Yellow, black-spotted body of a leopard.
   Tawny lion haunches on the fleet feet of a red deer.
   Meaningless and all too meaningful.

♔ ♔ ♔

LYNN SHUNNED her mother's book. It made Doris cry on Christmas morning. Awful. Doris lied later. Christmas dinner. Lied her tears were joy. Awful.

   When Silas read from the book, the boys invited onto his lap—Lynn never fell for it—or when Doris, reading sideways, her head resting on Silas's shoulder, Lynn damned them all in her heart. Liars.

   Doris asleep. The book open in her lap. The night Silas sends Lynn into her mother's sickroom. The night before the last night. Lynn wishes it had been the awful book her mother burned the night she hanged. Doris left it on her pillow. The Once and Future King. *The Kingston family curse.*

   "Lynn, it's foolish to hate a book." Doris.
   Lynn. "It's foolish to love a book about losers."

Set the dining table. Doris lays the linen. Lynn trails her clockwise around the round table, placing the silver.

Doris. "Just because everyone loses doesn't mean it's a book about losers."

Her mother's voice made music bland by comparison; Lynn misses her mother's tenor most painfully of all.

Doris says, "I like to think it's a book about the strength of wishes. When hope isn't strong enough. About how wishes that can't come true can—if we embrace them—define for us the furthest boundaries of truest faith. There must be some part of it you like."

There is. Lynn knows there is. Right off the top of her head.

Wordlessly, she swivels on her heel. Goes back. Counterclockwise. Removes knives from beside forks on their napkins. Places them beside the spoons on the other side of their respective plates. Doris, eternally patient, watches; amused and filled with love for her daughter's myriad expressions of faith in herself.

Lynn finishes. "In our family, we don't use them with the same hand."

"We don't. I think this is an agreeable change."

Lynn meets her mother's gaze.

"I like King Pellinore and the Questing Beast OK."

"Glatisant."

"It's the only part that's funny."

Doris. Patient for more. Lynn's imagination can't help but engage.

"You know, Mom. When King Pellinore falls in love with the daughter of the Netherlands king and he gives up questing after the Beast, and then his two friend-knights miss going out questing with him, so they

dress up like Glatisant. And then they get into trouble when the real Glatisant dragon falls in love with them. That's funny." Big grin.
  "It is funny. Thank you."

♔ ♔ ♔

TWO HOURS DOWN the Glatisant rabbit hole, Lynn knew one thing with certainty. Hundreds of thousands of people are obsessed with the Arthurian mythical beast and the stultifying passion they had for blogging, chatting, arguing over Glatisant in terms of books and movies; role-playing games and dice values; magic power card games; and table-top war games battled with miniature figurines; painting guides and what are official and non-official colors for said miniatures, and what characteristics those colors represented in "hit points." Refine, refine, refine—she minus signed them all. Discovered a dozen pages-worth of venues for Glatisant tattoos/t-shirts/coffee mugs—minus sign, minus sign, minus sign. After that, she discovered that in Switzerland, Geneva, there is a private bank.

Pell & Glatisant Trading Conglomerate, GmbH.

Discovered from their website that P&G Trading, like all private banking enterprises, gave out scant information. An address. A phone number, and what could only be called a warning: *Private Banking – By Appointment Only* that glaringly left out how one goes about securing said appointment.

Some quick side-searches ferreted out basic information: board/officers/regulatory standing—no one she'd ever heard, nothing of significance. She erased her search history.

Weak. Need to steal the device. Destroy it. Hardly perfect, but don't make it easy.

Put it on the bill. I've found your shadow, Michael. Reach-out-and-touch-you close.

Michael was in Switzerland. If he wanted Lynn to find him, he'd flash a signal. Leave a mark. Something Lynn could find. Something obscured from Langley.

From KALEIDOSCOPE. Kalaydoskop. From Silas.

What do I know?

Michael gave his cut-out a forgery of his Arthur Danford cover passport. Needed the original to travel Athens/Geneva. As far as Switzerland went, she could assume that anyone hunting him was already there. Michael would know that. Michael would go to ground.

Gary would know about Switzerland by now...unless he's already been denied. "Denied" equals Counterintelligence, equals Drexler. Equals personal vendetta. Watch out there.

Public lodging: out. Passport required. Passport registered.

Borrow a private room. Current/former assets/agents. In system—so, out.

A hook-up/one-night stand. Too risky to push more than overnight.

A hooker. Escape kit cash. Maybe buy him two/three nights. Any more: risk being sold out. No go.

Private residences. They can offer a room—student rooms, mostly. City permitted. Registration required. Out.

Small businesses sometimes offer workspace/single offices. Window-signed. Daily/weekly no city permit necessary. Find a lonely widow/older divorcée. Sweettalk. Cash. Hide his identity. For Michael—good as done.

Lynn didn't know his reason for pursuing P&G. Did she need it?

Ask Aiken? No. You're not his. He's not yours. He doesn't want you. Forget about Rusty—he'd have provided the intel if he had it. If he thought I needed it.

(Leigh. Tell him.)

Foolish. Focus.

Michael. A signal for his sister. How? Internet. How? A public message board/service website. One where you keep your identity disguised—the rule, not the exception. Dating site? No. Need a legit identity to set up an account. Arthur Danford—legit enough—compromised. Michael would go anonymous.

Old-school newspaper classified ad but modern electronic version. Somewhere massively crowded, where an innocuous message would instantly appear like a snowflake hitching a ride on an avalanche.

Where?

Sex worker site.

Michael tried that before. Once. A dead drop where he and his agent passed messages. But with the perv factor on one side, vice monitoring/regulating on the other, it was a total disaster. But as a dead-end, one-time flare fired into the black of cyberspace?

Since I hated it as soon as he suggested it and was proven right, Michael would remember. He was crazy about it. He never forgets or forgives when I call him out, and he loves flipping that kind of shit back on me. This time around? These circumstances? It'd be just about perfect.

Physical details—they all offer that—and something specific/unique/enticing. Something that would speak brother/sister, Michael to Lynn. Establish contact. Make a request. Take it from there.

Whir. Painkillers cycled.

The doctor had moved Lynn from oxycodone to tramadol. Substantially weaker. Still, it put her into a trance. Put her to sleep. The fog enveloped her. Lynn felt her being smile. Knew the wave of peace was, this time, genuine.

3.

THE LEVEL OF GRAVITAS Silas Kingston ascribed to CIA Director Jeremy Harker III was exemplified by the luncheon selection Harker made and now tossed in his mouth with his fingers. Popcorn shrimp. Silas ordered the rainbow trout. Said, "Not much more on the golf course. Are you these days?"

"And, my wife took sole proprietorship of our three dance studios," said Harker, and popped another, enjoying himself. "Still get my cardio in."

Silas pinned the fish's head, spoon behind the gills. Slid his knife beneath the flesh and down its spine. The dead eye wept.

Harker swallowed. "Really, it would surprise you how alike golf and dance are. When I'm on 850 maple-flex dance floor, I can't say I miss the links."

"That wouldn't surprise me. Though, there is one significant difference between dance and golf."

Harker raised an eyebrow while his eyes tracked the fish head, skeleton, and tail Silas transferred to the bone plate.

"No one famous was ever strangled to death on a golf course," said Silas.

Taken aback, but not about to voice a lack of ballroom knowledge, Harker popped another shrimp.

"Some famous female dancer." Silas delicately removed a bone from between his lips. "Afterward, you'll notice Fred Astaire never worked wearing a scarf again."

They ate in silence. Silas waited for Harker to fill the gap.

"I only asked you here to gloat. You thought you beat me—Operation ATROPOS and all that—but ultimately, I beat you."

"Jeremy. What happened between us wasn't personal. You got too close to things you knew nothing about."

Harker bristled. Silas smiled politely.

"After that," Harker went on, "I always wondered how you'd gotten to where you had at the top of the food chain, but when I wanted to look, I was already gone. I'm not ashamed to admit it, but one of the first things I did on my return was dig this up."

He patted Silas's personnel record, which had been staring at Silas since they'd seated and that Silas had blatantly ignored.

"You were almost tossed out of here, your first posting. Your entire first year in Moscow was a disaster. The young wife. The pregnancy you tried to hide instead of sending her home. Not a single recruitment. You rode two assets too hard. Trying to make up ground. Lost time. Succeeded in getting them rolled right up. Lubyanka shot is what we got back."

"I was there. Yes."

"And yet we kept you."

Silas lifted his wineglass. A mock toast.

"I admit," Harker went on. "I would have as well. Colonel Bogdon Ogievich of the Soviet Air Force Long Range Aviation branch. One of the most important recruitments we ever made."

Silas drank. Dabbed his mouth. Said, "Ironically, while we were building up our strategic long-range bombing capacity, the Cold War reinforced a shift in Soviet nuclear doctrine. Relied more heavily than we did on the creation of the Strategic Rocket Force, which assumed the major responsibility for transporting ICBMs towards America. Contrary to our doctrine for nuclear engagement with long-range aircraft, the primary goal of the Soviet Air Force Long Range Aviation branch was a smaller, more nimble theater-level force capable of delivering both nuclear and conventional bomb loads on NATO countries within Europe at a moment's notice. Until I recruited Colonel Ogievich, we were blind to the plans and protocols, distribution of warhead munitions, the codes and targeting lists required to successfully observe, understand, and disrupt this threat.

"It was a lunch in Tula, not unlike this one, where I turned him—though the whole thing almost worked out disastrously for me. My predecessor in counterintelligence, James Jesus Angleton—"

"I'm well aware of who your predecessor was. And why do you compare these two lunches? I must say, I don't like the insinuation."

"Bear with me. Angleton was certain I'd been doubled. Colonel Ogievich was taken away from me. I was yanked—along with my young wife and newborn son—back home, and I was put through hell by CI."

A waiter cleared plates.

Harker took up the conversational ball right where Silas had left it for him: "Only to become Angleton's protégé and, after he left, the most successful chief of Counterintelligence we ever had. You helped bring down Aldrich Ames."

"I don't like traitors."

"No. Bad for business, I like to say."

Silas pointed the waiter—now waiting with coffee—to fill his china cup. Another wait. Silas: "You do like secrets. Yes?"

"I'm the Director of the CIA. I know them all. So, in a sense, they're rather common, mundane."

"Then let me tell you the reason I'm here. I've held a secret. Many years. It isn't revealed to all directors—not in its entirety. I will reveal it to you in exchange for a return to active status."

"I'm not sure I'm believing you right now."

"I've steamrolled you before. I'm happy to do it again. Is that what you want? Because I never fuck around. Ever. Yes, or no?"

Harker was thoughtful. "No—" caught himself, hands flapping up like a pair of nervous pigeons. "I mean, 'No, you don't fuck around.' Should have begun with 'Yes.' Definitely."

"You must be, at the very least, *familiar* with KALEI-DOSCOPE."

Harker went still. "Mr. Kingston. You must know I can't speak to that."

"No. You can't. But I can change that for you."

A weird man. Odd quirks and personal interests. Harker was not a stupid man, nor was he a foolish man, as his peculiarities and addiction to spite led others to believe.

"You. How long?"

Silas regarded him with a close-lipped disposition; the look of a smile that wasn't really a smile; a facial expression nature perfected with reptiles. "I came to the Agency from that other body. Took the reins in time to coincide with our nation's bicentennial. To discuss this further, we'll need to remove to the SCIF."

Harker did not answer right away. Silas finished his first fish. Waited to begin reeling in his next.

♔ ♔ ♔

AFTER MIDNIGHT, Director Harker joined Mrs. Harker in bed. They made love, and if either of them smoked, they would have lit up like couples once did in movies to tell the audience—Hey, these two just got it on. Harker had had no nicotine. Was giddy anyway. Announced to his wife that it was Isadora Duncan—she was the famous dancer strangled by her scarf. But, get this, she *wasn't* dancing. The end of her scarf blew out her car window and caught on the wheel axle.

"September 14, 1927. And, for your edification, Fred Astaire doesn't star in a dance musical until *Flying Down to Rio* in 1933. Wore scarves many times in many movies after that."

And yet, after tossing and turning all night with bad dreams of Silas Kingston strangling him at Arthur Murray, Harker's first order of business was to have a security team check his three studios and put up an order for ongoing/intermittent surveillance. He was Director of the Central Intelligence Agency. The most powerful intelligence organization in the world. It paid to be careful.

After that, he made notes on a work-up soon for the President's Daily Brief. How in the hell does a high-value detainee—a violent and dangerous terrorist—interrogated in Poland pursue a lawsuit against us ten years later out of his cell in Guantanamo Bay?

If they'd left me in charge, this would never see the light of day. Now all I do is clean up the other guy's mess.

His fingers burrowed beneath his glasses. Massaged the bridge of his nose. Thought about pipelines and energy dominance and the picture/reality Silas Kingston had painted for him. A fair-play/eyes-open/politics-free brand of intelligence older and saner than the Agency had ever dreamed.

♕ ♕ ♕

MOMENTS PAST three in the morning, Lynn struck gold. Better, hopped the neighbor's wall and plucked an orange. She'd run her search nine hours with only a thirty-minute doze midway. She'd excluded premium sites. Membership sites. "Model" Agency sites. Excluded hotel-licensed call girls/guys. Excluded high-end escorts. Excluded fetish. Focused straight—male and female. Wasted two hours on a Craigslist-type site—too random/too temp/too un-shielded personal. Swiss-leaning: excluded. EU-centric: excluded. American-exclusive: excluded. Isolated international-geared porn video/plus cameras/plus classifieds. Excluded amateur upload sites (or she'd be at this for the rest of her life).

Found: sexxxtravaganza.oui.su. Impulse—searched "red hair." Found: "Artsy Dani." Found headline: *"Climb the wall. Taste the oranges."*

Nice bimbo cleavage shot. Gutter mind Michael.

But I gotcha.

Lynn allowed her excitement to linger. Watched her heart rate and blood pressure spike. Pound a minute. Proud a minute.

Michael, you glorious son-of-a-bitch.

Worked her tube. Calmed with air. The rest of the profile: *"Ride like a Mustang. Gorgeous apartment overlooking park. Want to go slow. Happy to meet via a cup of coffee. Leave message."*

Unpack it. Artsy/Dani/Mustang. Arthur Dan Ford. Wants to "go slow." No question mark. It's a request. Meet via cup of coffee. Coffee cup: concealment device. Dead drop: the park. Which park?

Lynn studied Artsy Dani's contact info.

Email: SweetRed46.207027@sexxxtravaganza.oui

Mobile: 41.22.616.7987

Didn't need to test them. Didn't matter whether they went random or backstopped anywhere. These weren't address/phone numbers. Lynn opened a new browser window.

Map program. Entered: *46.207027.* Dropped the 41 country/22 city codes. Entered: *6.167987.*

GPS coordinates. The map zoomed. Europe, Switzerland. Zoom Geneva. Zoomed Parc la Grange. Zoomed to a pin drop on a walking trail through thick woods.

Lynn couldn't zoom in further, but visualized a trash receptacle. A dead drop waiting with/for a coffee cup message. All she had to do now was get out of this hospital and get to Foxtail Farm.

Friday, July Ninth
1.

F OR LYNN, GETTING OUT of the hospital was like that kid's song about the green grass hole in the ground. Hole in the ground, root in the hole, the tree on the root. Her version? A litany of risks and refusals and threats, adding one on top of the other. Risk of infection. Risk of re-opening your wound. Risk of losing your breathing. Life risk. Goes against hospital post-surgical policy. Violates terms of care you signed. Invalidates your insurance coverage. Federal government covering the insurance gap has legal authority. Legal responsibility. Ongoing criminal investigation. But, like the song, the whole thing stemmed from a hole, and that hole was a hole in Lynn's f-ing throat. So, *adios*.

As though suffering far greater pain than Lynn's own, the hospital agreed to release Lynn Kingston upon medical evaluation and her signature on a legal form waiving her rights to sue for complications arising from the early discharge.

The form would be ready by 2:00 p.m. The evaluation: scheduled for 4:00 p.m—which would be when Lynn would receive her prescriptions. Lynn didn't bother typing out "fuck it" and was out the door by noon.

Dr. Goldfarb came outside looking for her. She tried to warn him off with dour eyes. He joined her while she waited in a wheelchair for her ride.

"You'll need help," he said. Wrote on his jotter. "Just because your feeding tube is out, you'll need help preparing food, and eating. Caring for your P/M valve. Your wound and your dressing will need constant monitoring. Proper cleaning. Changing." He tore out a piece of paper.

Lynn typed: *Why are you being nice to me?*

"I'm worried about you. It's a serious wound. Anyone else would have lost you on the table." He winked. Handed her the paper. "But I watch the news. Read some. You're in a serious business. I can't imagine your decision to leave us has been taken lightly. Remember Janella? Your night nurse. Left for vacation."

Lynn opened the paper. *Janella Jenkins* and a telephone number.

"We've spoken. Says I'm twisting her arm, but she'll cancel her vacation to Boring-Boring. Have someone call and make the arrangements?"

Lynn nodded. A loud muffler'd, loud red Dodge Ram stopped before her.

"I'd like to look at you at my private practice in a week. Janella knows how to find me. Good luck, Ms. Kingston."

Hal came around the truck. "And how is this not your worst idea? Ever?"

Lynn pointed at the tracheostomy valve in her throat. Gave a smug grimace. Typed on her tablet. Showed him.

I'm sending you to Michael. We're on a ticking clock. Good to go?

A raised eyebrow. "Always. Off the books?"

Lynn: *Entirely. And no Silas.* She locked eyes with him. Deep serious. Typed/showed: *This op could cost you.*

"Old man's already pushed that on me. Happy to give him a poke in the eye right back."

❦ ❦ ❦

PROACTIVE. Time scaled fast for Lynn. For Hal. Forty minutes to North Bethesda. Lynn's Rock Creek Terrace condominium tower. Would stay at Foxtail Farm, duration of their op. Sent Hal up for her clothes.

"How you want me to do that?"

Lynn typed: *Squeamish about my underwear drawer?*

"Yeah. So what?"

Typed: *Trash bag under kitchen sink. Laundry room. Dirty clothes basket. Fill the bag.*

She gave him the combo to her safe. Lynn: *Zipper bag. Leave passport. Leave gun. Bring cash.*

Ticking clock. Two supermarkets. Two shopping plazas. Two strip malls. Hopscotching back south to D.C. Cash for pre-paid credit cards. Two AMEX: $5,000 each. Two Visa: $1,000 each. Seven Mastercard: $500 a pop. Each stop, seat cranked back—engine on, air conditioning on—Lynn rested.

Ticking clock. Arlington Walmart, Arlington Target. Arlington Costco: twenty-two SIM cards. Cash. 6:00 p.m. Pentagon Centre Best Buy—cash—two prepaid phones. Fifteen minutes—out of the lot onto Hayes Street, medium traffic—straight shot into Reagan National.

Arrivals parking. Lynn: the truck. Hal: baggage claim. One phone/SIM card each. Activated. Signals caught/buried in the busiest cell tower in Virginia. Hal dialed Lynn. Lynn connected. Tapped the horn. Hal headed back to the truck. Driving. One hour west. Lynn: each phone/$1k extra data purchase. Spent Visa cards out the window. Ticking clock. Dulles. International. Outbound.

Gunshot. Scissors. Michael/not Michael carousel'd around.

Bury it. Hole in the ground.

Lynn focused. The two Amex. Typed: *France, Italy, Austria?*

"I can call in a favor out of Milan. We trained—six, seven years back—with their Lagunari Regiment. He's retired. Won't ask questions." Off Lynn's dubious look, Hal—"It's an enormous debt."

Lynn typed: *Flight out*— She handed him the first AMEX. Second AMEX: *Flight back.* The stack of MasterCards. *Seven days and out. One for each day. No matter what. End of day—balance or no balance: toss it.* Hard look.

Hal said, "No matter what." She offered the rest of the SIMs. Hal took the chips.

Lynn typed: *The one in your phone now. That's for any data/intel Michael passes you. And a failsafe in case the others don't work.*

"Which I use—"

Each is a one-use comms link between us.

"Why do I get the feeling I'm not bringing Michael back with me?"

He didn't ask.

"So we're just support."

Support in !!!ALL FORMS!!! The all-knowing look between them. She typed out the details on his presumed dead drop. Hal memorized, helped his sister from the passenger side to the driver's seat. He held her hand.

"Tell Melody I got called on business. She'll know. And you—" He pointed at her wound/the PM valve. "Get back in the hospital or get a Darth Vader helmet. You look like a freak."

Lynn blew a kiss off her middle finger and watched until he disappeared inside the terminal.

NOTHING WAS PLEASANT that night around Doris Kingston's dining room table. The candles burned weaker. The mirrors made little effort to return any glow. Unhappiness over no news on Michael's disappearance. Unhappiness over Hal snatched away on "business." No one was happy that Lynn had checked herself out of the hospital in defiance of her doctors and her insurance. Melody served comfort food. Spaghetti and meatballs, garlic bread. The twins, Charlotte, and Leigh loved it—dinner on TV trays. DVD on the porch.

Silas closed the glass doors between the dining room and the kids. "Where's Paige?"

"She's having dinner with her new friend," said Gwen.

"Boyfriend?" Silas sought confirmation.

"I think she flatters herself. He's too old for her to be serious."

"And yet you're grinning like the cat."

Gwen waited for him to finish. Then, "What? 'Who ate the canary?'"

"I didn't mention any birds. You couldn't catch one if it fell asleep between your paws. Just the cat."

He took a bite of food. Aimed the tines of his empty fork at Lynn. "And you're lucky you can't speak because you would fail at any explanation you offered. I'm having you returned to the hospital tomorrow."

Lynn set aside the protein smoothie Melody had prepared for her. Machine-gunned her fingers across her keypad. Shared it.

Don't bother. I've hired a nurse. Melody is setting us up in your former master suite.

Melody added, "It was her night nurse from the hospital. She's entirely capable and has graciously chosen to work here, caring for Lynn, over her vacation week."

Silas frowned. "The hospital won't allow it."

Lynn typed: *1. Hospital did. 2. State of Maryland does. 3. Tough luck—you.*

Silas reconsidered his food. "Fast-fingered gal. You missed your calling as a secretary. Back in the day." Stabbed a meatball. Grumbled. "Your house, Melody. As you wish. And Gwen—ah, how quaint; still smirking—I saw your suitcases." Fork as royal trident.

"Your granddaughters and I hope to stay until Michael's situation has more clarity—hopefully, safely on his way home."

"I see. And you find humor in all this. Why?"

"Not humor. I'm just happy." Like clockwork, better—waterworks—her eyes grew moist. "It's been very hard, this last posting, for Michael and me." She looked to each of her sisters-in-law as if recruiting a team. "We thought we'd gotten to the end of things. We went so far as beginning divorce proceedings."

Lynn and Melody leaned back from Gwen's team table-edge sideline to share their bafflement behind her.

Silas finished chewing. Twirled noodles with his fork. "You *did* go through a divorce."

Gwen's smile lost its vitality. Her lips clenched. She made a strange sound. Mewing would be the word.

"What was that?" Silas speared another meatball.

"I don't know how you could possibly know that—"

"Of course you don't."

"But that said..." She reached down; took a document from her purse.

Silas held out his hand. Gwen hesitated.

Silas: "Whatever it is, I won't tear it in two."

Gwen, hand trembling, clearly now feared he would.

"Gwen," Silas soothed. "One doesn't produce—what would you call that? Some sort of 'a-ha' evidence—and not share it to prove its validity, which you have now, in hesitation, made questionable."

Gwen folded it. Tucked it away. "Forget it."

"Also. This is not a bus depot. No need here for women's cosmetic bags or carry-ons."

Gwen finger-swiped her eyelids.

Melody said, "Silas, sometimes your 'joking voice' doesn't come through as clearly as you intend it to. Gwen, go on. It sounded like you had good news."

"Before the incident in Turkey, Michael and I had a 'meeting of hearts.' That document Silas was so entirely rude about, and mean and mocking, was Michael's signed affidavit for a reversal of the divorce." She let her eyes go. Happy tears, whether they belong to a woman or an alligator, or a cat, allow sparkle. "It's like heaven shined down on us before these other awful events. Love conquers all!" (A little hip-hip-hooray cheerleader pantomime to help her case), and, "I submit it to the court tomorrow."

"Good luck with that."

"You're merciless!" Her voice cracked. She threw her napkin. Rose defiantly. Teetered on her heels. "I'll tell you this, you psycho. As soon as Michael's spousal pay starts coming in, I am taking my girls, and we are out of this insane asylum until Michael returns—alive or dead!" She lifted her chin. Elevated her chest. Looked to Melody— "I don't typically like spaghetti, but thank you for dinner." And to Lynn— "I'm sorry, Lynn. I know how much your relationship with *all* your nieces means to you, but this whole dynamic needs a change."

Lynn typed: *Dynamic!*

Silas considered Gwen with gentle eyes. "But the suitcases. For now, we can count on you staying?"

They all knew. Not even a question.

"I will be watching *Mulan* with the children."

The other three waited for the French doors to close behind her.

Melody dipped her chin so she could give Silas the upward eyes. "I hope you're happy. Especially after what you put Hal through this morning."

"Hal did as he was told."

Lynn typed: *What???*

Melody: "Hal changed his statement to lie and say he saw Michael killed."

Lynn typed: *What does that get but trouble for Hal?* Pointed eyes, sharp at Silas.

"I am sure what you've pushed him into is far worse," the old man parried. "And, okay, I tease too hard with Gwen. I don't like her when Michael is not around. Idle hands wear glue-on fingernails."

"Be honest—" Melody again. "You don't really like her when he is around. You don't like Gwen at all, and that's sad."

"I love my son, and I love my granddaughters. And they love her."

"We *all* love her."

Lynn gave a little shrug. She didn't. Melody ignored.

Silas went on. "With Hal's report, there won't be any money for her to run off with. Our family—*loving* family—will remain intact. And I promise you, Melody, I will be nicer from now on."

He twisted more spaghetti, stabbed, and ate another meatball. Pointed his fork at Lynn. "You, Missy, better know what you're doing and do it right. I can't bother to run behind you and clean up all your messes."

Strangled, unpleasant laughter escaped Lynn's valve. She typed: *On what imagined authority?*

"I'm returning to work. Keep me less underfoot around here."

He searched, knife and fork, for one last meatball. None remained. Lynn typed. Showed it to Melody. She smirked. Lifted the serving bowl. "Lynn says, 'We're out of canary.'"

FIGHTING EXHAUSTION, fighting pain, the voice in her head screamed she should go back to the hospital, now that Hal was en route. Lynn slumped in a kitchen chair pulled up beside the counter. Loaded dishes and utensils Melody rinsed into the dishwasher.

"I wish you'd just let me do this."

Lynn typed: *I wish you'd hire kitchen help.*

"I don't read much. I don't like television. The boys get way enough of me all day." She held a plate out of Lynn's reach to draw her eyes to her face. "This is where I excel and where I show my gratitude to the rest of you." She handed over the plate. "I can't hug you as much as I hug the kids."

Lynn: *Most of the time, we're a sorry lot to be grateful for.*

"Neither of us believes that."

The tablet: *AND you show too much of it—and kindness—with Silas. I TOLERATE Gwen and her nonsense, but I don't completely disagree with her on the old "psycho" bit.*

"I know. And that comes from *your* experience." She bypassed Lynn's waiting hand as she loaded glassware into the upper rack. "My experience with Silas has always been of kindness and generosity."

He treats you like a princess.

Amused, Melody struck a regal pose. Lynn shared her grin. Typed.

He's dangerous. Be careful. It didn't work out for our— Lynn caught herself. Tried to backspace her way out of it.

"Your mother?"

Typed: *Embarrassed. Sorry.*

"Tell me about the mirrors. Did Doris collect them? Or did both of them? Or...?"

I don't know, really. It started before I was born. I think both of them. But he went overboard with it during her cancer and after.

"I wonder what he's hoping to see."

He's set them so that it's always her.

"Sometimes even after you close the door and block the stairway, huh?"

She wasn't looking for a response. Lynn considered her faraway look. Melody retreated from ghosts. Addressed her directly. "Whatever secret you and Silas keep burning between yourselves, he despises himself for it."

Typed. *Not how he expresses it to me.*

Melody added soap. Closed the dishwasher door. Lynn typed: *Could I get you to rinse this, please? Hot water and soap.* She unscrewed her valve. Melody took it in her hand.

"How long do you have this? The hole closes, right?"

About two weeks after the tube comes out. And "Yes." Should be good as new.

"That makes me happy." She turned up the hot water. A brush and some soap. Said, "Don't you think it's exactly—the 'despisedness,' if that's a word—what he's expressing to you? It's all out of fear." She returned

Lynn's valve. "Fear if you get close, you'll turn out like that secret part of him he sacrificed and can't escape."

Lynn attempted to fasten her P/M valve. Gave Melody a mirthless grin before—*He never sacrificed a thing in his life. That man's selfishness knows no boundaries.*

She exposed her throat to Melody, who leaned in and examined. "Looks good to me—like it did when you got here. Lynn, somewhere, sometime, Silas broke himself. Like you would a stick." She mimicked the snapping with her fists. "From his own family. He lives every minute of every day on the outside from the rest of us. Like some banished character from the kids' DVDs. I think—and don't let this annoy you too much; it's just what *I* think. I think he pushes and pushes at you; he pushes you away because you're the only one who can bring him back."

Fury exploded in Lynn's face.

Melody softly finished. "He's terrified of that."

Lynn ripped out a message on her pad. *He should be. Because one day, I'm going to kill him for it.*

Torment and hostility radiated from Lynn; her heartbeat pulsed at her temple.

"Lynn. I can see this is real with you. I get it. I can't tell you in strong enough words the toll that would take on you would be worse than—"

Lynn smacked letters on the tablet. *I'm willing to give up my freedom. And if it costs my life, I don't care. Happy with it.*

"You know I'm not talking about that cost."

A bitter, *fuck-it* smirk. Typed: *Mom's birthday—one of these years. Make sure to be there for the party. Sis.*

Not something you answer. Melody held her with her eyes—openness, concerned sympathy, a willingness to honesty—but Lynn was done. Took her tablet. Gone.

Melody blew a long breath of air, giving it sound. Like a mournful wind building, blowing back at her from so many birthdays of her own.

My wish: Daddy stops hurting Mama when he drinks his poison. So, God, you *kill him. I don't want to have to.*

Whoosh! Birthday wishes extinguished.

Melody's phone interrupted her thoughts. A text from an unknown Arkansas number. Melody didn't believe in coincidence; she knew things about the forces of darkness. She clutched her phone, her palm covering the message notification.

She moved methodically. Pushed Lynn's chair back to the table. Placed Lynn's tablet on the table's surface. She shut off the lights and went to the swinging door. Pushed into the kitchen hallway.

Melody advanced through the dim light, refusing to look into the mirrors. To let Doris affect her in re-flection. Through the front parlor. Onto the stairway landing. She faced Doris's portrait. Tapped open the message. Held it up to the dead woman's dancing eyes.

2.

*L*YING ON THE GRASS. *The crowns of their heads touch. Like the center post of a clock. Their bodies stretch away from each other. His legs, the long hand. Her's the short. Set at three o'clock, which, although done unconsciously, reflects the hour of this conversation.*

"I don't understand. You're painting me inside a room. At night. You said, an arched window with black sky and stars over my shoulder." Doris wears the gown depicted in the portrait. Replicated in Boone's pastel and charcoal study sketches—strewn around them:

Doris turning in the sunlight. Red sequins agleam; Doris leaning back, letting heavenly fire burnish her sequined decolletage; Doris's hands stretched forward, shoulders arched, casting shadow on her breast, while light blazes waist to knee.

"Yes," Boone answered. "A ballroom. And not a drop of moonlight. Only stars. A party. A dance. Only you can see it. We don't know—never will be sure—if you're stepping into it, or stepping away; if you love your guests or you're mocking them..."

"I love it. I do. But the shiny, shimmery sunlight seems wrong."

"It's a trick." He picked a seed stalk of grass. He tickled her cheek. "I'm painting the light coming off you—not coming on—coming from. Coming out. You are sunlight emergent."

She laughs. Swats at the teasing grass. It is a laugh like merry birds. Like bells. A laugh like fire might make if fuel and heat were made of life. "Boone—what do you do with light—I mean, it seems somewhat unfair—with a woman who commissions a portrait already set outdoors?"

He twirls the seed stalk above his eyes. "Picture the brightest, fiercest summer day."

"Ahhh..."

"Now, in your mind's eye, lay snow upon the ground. See that extra sparkle. That's what I would capture."

"It would take a long time to work on that painting. And cold."

"No, it's only in my imagination; I've not yet met the woman. Just the snow. The dazzling snow. The woman who is that dazzling—I don't know her yet."

Doris flops her arm, a backhand slap across his chest. "Thanks heaps."

He holds it. Strokes the underside of her bare forearm once. She pulls away. He takes it back. A slow caress. Kisses it.

"You know, you're doing a better job at seducing me out here than you were indoors. And you'll need to stop."

Boone rises, sitting on his haunches, pulling up his knees. He looks between them. "I'm ashamed of myself. I'm so sorry, Mrs. Kingston."

"Keep with 'Doris.' You'll only ruin this." She peers at him, trying to catch his eye with a sympathetic smile. "I'm having a blast. We're just fine without the other."

"You had nothing to do with it. My fault totally."

"Shut up. Relax. I'm the one who had the bright idea to flash you." She sits up, eagerly. "I know what we can do. Might help inspire your creativity."

"What's that?"

"We'll trade secrets." A gesture to the main manor behind her. "Something about the house my portrait will hang inside of."

Boone grins. Leans back on an elbow. Withdraws a sterling silver flask. Capped, he gestures with it. "You've caught my attention."

"In the 1600s, two Kingston brothers built Foxtail Farm. It was to be for both their families."

"But...?"

"One, my husband's ancestor, killed the other in a duel."

"Wonderful. Over a woman, I'm sure you'll tell me."

"That is the accepted story. However, Silas told me, when we first moved in, it was not over a woman. It was over the slave trade. With tobacco, the one brother considered it a necessary evil."

She studies his face, her eyes beneath a knitted brow.

"Uh-oh," says Boone.

"Uh-oh is right. Slavery continued after the duel. Our wharf was where most slaves for the colony arrived and—Silas didn't tell me this—but you can find it at the historical society. There was a notorious slave hunter. An Indian named John Turkey, or something. Apparently, once a slave himself. He was foreman here. Slaves

that escaped—not just from here, but all over—who needed discipline, or a final solution, came to Foxtail Farm. Brought to him. The original Silas's right-hand man. None ever left."

"That's a fucking awful story. Doris. You know that my wife is of the African-American race."

All emotion leaves Doris's face. "You weren't thinking of your wife when you were kissing my arm."

Boone dry swallows. Notices his thirst. Unscrews his flask. His hand shakes. He drinks.

"I want that in my portrait. That's who's at the dance." She sniffs the air. "What is that awful smell? Is it paint thinner?"

"Absinthe. Mixed with linseed oil and turpentine."

"Why?"

"It takes me places. Deep places. My art flows through me. I can't explain, but I won't stop."

She watches him drink more.

"You realize, Boone, I have nothing to do with that history. Neither does my husband."

"My wife would want to see all this burned to the ground."

Doris lets the sunshine back in; laughs it back out. She locks her eyes with his. "Maybe one day," she says, taking his flask. Takes a sip. She puckers her mouth. Covers it with the back of her wrist until, gasping, says, "I told you mine. You tell me yours."

Boone stares at her in disbelief. He sees a droplet of the vile liquid on her exquisite lips. He licks his own. As if to taste it. Takes another belt. Goes gruff.

"I could never be unfaithful. I was just playing around."

"That didn't seem like acting."

Voice raw from the chemicals. "I was playing, because I knew you'd reject me."

"You're a famous—a great—artist. Others don't reject you, I imagine."

"I make sure they do."

"How strange."

He belts another.

"I have to stay faithful to my wife."

"Why, Boone?"

Glug-glugs another.

"Because she's unfaithful to me. And here's my secret." He leans in, his eyes bloodshot and crazy and serious. "I'm going to kill her for it."

Doris stares at him. Her eyes match his for seriousness. Then she laughs. "Boone! That was better than mine. When you do, I am sure you will cement your place in history as the great and tragic portraitist."

He grins back. "Better than cutting off an ear to spite your face."

The humor they share, in this moment, is dreadfully false in both. Doris gingerly takes his flask. He watches, hopeful she drinks more deeply this time. Doris screws on the cap.

"This stuff will kill you before you get recognition for any of it."

"Only after it drives me mad. Until then—maybe then—I want to cement my name painting from that edge."

Seduction.

Madness.

Murder.

Poison.

A woman, yet unknown, dazzling in the snow that isn't there.

Doris shudders. Doris stands. Doris turns in the sunlight, dazzling the red sequins. "This dress is so gorgeous. I could be on a runway in Paris."

"It's a Paul Poiret Art Deco dropped waistline sheathe dress. Like one in the collection of the Metropolitan Museum of Art. The red, though, I had my wife do—she made it."

"She's very talented. This is the most lovely dress I've ever worn. Would it be okay if we paid her for it? I don't think I'll want to let it go."

Boone stands. He moves around her. He finds an angle. He says, "Don't move. This is exactly what I'm seeking." As he sketches, he says, "Your husband is giving you the portrait for your birthday. My gift to you is the dress."

Doris watches the sunlight sparkle and dance over her breasts and down her waist. She feels the strangeness of the absinthe and the other poisons and warms at the memories of how her real seduction felt exactly this way.

♚ ♚ ♚

PAIGE RETURNED to Foxtail Farm at ten minutes after ten that night to find the manor house shuttered for bed. Although the house was dark, she felt light pouring out of her.

I'm the girl in the song. In every song. In love. It's amazing: I'm in love, I'm in love—with a kind, smart, movie-star-beautiful, mmm, hot-ass spy man.

She whispered it in her mind to all her reflections in all the mirrors she floated past. Paused when she noticed that, in the darkness of the mirrors, she inexplicitly appeared cocooned in an aura of light. The hair on her arms snapped to attention. She noticed the light's source. Moonlight through the high stairwell windows beamed through the glass and illuminated her grandmother's portrait. The colored oil gleamed. Glistened. It was Doris's light, and Paige spun happily to find her.

Paige giggled. "I'm in love with a British spy. What do you say to that?" And she stretched her arms high, fingers spread. Did a happy dance. She stretched her arms higher. Reached across space and time to her grandmother's image, aglow/alive in moonlight. "If you don't tell, I won't either!"

I'm in love and I'm giving him all that God made of me.

Paige didn't notice, but a cloud passed over the moon. The light remained the same.

♔ ♔ ♔

OUT THE CUSTOMS cattle chute, international arrival lobby, Milan's Malpensa Airport. Hal. Flight tired. Late-afternoon hot. The Italian circled the American unnoticed. Came up behind. Swiftly. Defter and stealthier than you'd expect a guy this size. Swung an elbow and forearm as thick as Hal's calf into the center of Hal's back. More surprisingly, Hal braced at the shock and took it standing firm. Without turning, said, "Stuff any guns in your mouth recently?"

"Your wife know you're still gay?"

Hal chuckled. Turned. Major Pietro Vianello, retired from the Lagunari Regiment, grinned. Displayed a startling, triangular gap where his top two front teeth once met. Said, "Eight years, I'm waiting for you to fix my teeth."

"See a dentist. Anyway, the kids you wouldn't have if I hadn't knocked that gun out of your fist wouldn't recognize you if you suddenly became handsome."

Hal thrust out his hand. Pietro took it. Tugged him in. Kissed his cheeks. Held him back to look at him like a mother inspecting her schoolboy. A big mother. Height-wise, Pietro edged him out by two inches. Also had about twenty-five pounds more muscle than Hal and anyone else in the neighborhood. The neighborhood being the entire city. Hal fit, with room to spare, in his shadow.

Pietro pistol-shot a finger at the doors. "Car fueled and ready to go. Should take three-and-a-half, four hours."

"So, let's go."

Friends now, they hadn't been from the start. Certainly, hadn't chosen one another. A joint training US/Italian riverine exercise back in 2004. Macho, show-off shit. Excuse for the brass to party in Venice. The pair of them partnered up for the two weeks, billeted together in a room meant for one at the regiment's headquarters in Mestres. Never hit it off. Nothing specific—happens a lot, these sorts of things—temperament/rivalry/resentment. Less than cordial. More than cold. Do the work, make the best of it, stay out of each other's way.

Hal had no earthly idea why, on their last night, awarded a pass into Venice to raise a glass to the successful completion of the exercise, he'd turned around and gone back to their room to invite Pietro to tag along. One second-thought, one second slower, the elevator rather than bounding the stairs, Pietro would have never gotten around to purchasing the Alfa Romeo GTV they were blasting up the A4 toward the Great St. Bernard Pass. He'd have been dead. Hal caught Pietro off guard the moment the Italian clamped his teeth on the barrel of the Beretta and thumbed off the safety. Hal lunged. Knocked the pistol and half of Pietro's front teeth to the floor. Both men followed the trajectory of the weapon as it bounced on the floor and clattered into the wall. Shared a look of relief it didn't discharge, before humiliation filled the Italian's face.

Hal sat beside him. Put an arm around his boulder back. Leaned around. Grinned in his face. Gave him a shake and said, "I owe you a drink."

"Why?"

"You just made my night."

"Some American hero."

"Fuck that. Better. You weren't an asshole 'cause you hated me. All this time, you were being an asshole because you hated yourself."

Pietro lumbered to the pistol. Made it safe. Put it on the desk. Laid his hand on it and said, "How do you know this broken heart of mine wasn't *all* about you?"

Pietro deadpanned.

Hard to say who burst out laughing first. That night, they got uproariously drunk.

Pre-dawn gray, Hal pummeled the apartment door belonging to Pietro's unfaithful girlfriend until her father answered. Unperturbed. *"Bianca! Il tuo cane randagio è tornato!"* *Bianca! Your stray dog is back!* He smirked at Pietro. *"Dalle un minute perché il suo ragazzo esca dalla finestra."* *Give her a minute for her boyfriend to climb out the window.*

Pietro paled. Hal didn't understand. Didn't care. Leaned past the father and shouted up the stairs. "Bianca! Get your ass down here! Front and center!"

And she did.

"Your proper boyfriend here almost killed a man over you last night. Now he's got something to say."

Hal stepped back as Pietro drunkenly confessed his profound and eternal love for Bianca. Got on his knees. Halfway through his proposal, the cringing new boyfriend came up behind Bianca. Tried to touch her. She swatted his hand away and Hal threw him like a paper airplane into the street. He sailed away. By the time Hal turned back, Bianca had collected her drunken soldier and was shooing Hal away.

Eight months later, Hal received email photos. Pietro, Bianca, and a baby bump from their honeymoon in the Seychelles.

"You ever tell her?" Hal asked as they crossed the frontier into Switzerland without incident.

"No. But she knew. Told me on the night before our first was born. She said, 'I might think twice about marrying a man who killed another man for my hand. Anyone can kill out of jealousy or rage. But the man who would commit the worst kind of murder at all—prefer eternity in hell than face losing me—that's a man whose hand I'll never release until we reach heaven's gate.'"

Pietro left Hal in the parking lot for the Genève-Pâquis ferry. Before Hal left his car, Peitro gave him a SIG Sauer P220.

"Traceable?"

Pietro shook his head. "Spare parts from decommissioned pieces I collected over the years from the armory." He handed Hal a suppressor. "This is mine. Don't wear it out."

Hal watched him drive away. Set off, on foot, across the Pont du Mont Blanc bridge. Headed for an appointment with a coffee cup.

Saturday, July Tenth
1.

LYNN WOULD HAVE SPIRITED him away. Wrung him out like a dishrag in the sink of some cookie-cutter anonymous safe house; Hal would have just killed the man. But Michael was a people person from way back. While it was true, his ability as a case officer to engage, captivate, and persuade individuals to find new purpose for their lives, appealing to their vanity, their pocketbooks, or baser, more devilish desires, his charms focused on their betraying their birthright—the theft of national secrets—to the point of treason. In the case of Antonio Abbatantuono, President/CEO, Pell & Glatisant Trading Conglomerate, GmbH, Michael hadn't a clue what secrets he needed this man to betray. For that, they would have to speak.

Three days surveillance. Abbatantuono kept a strict routine. Arrive (one black-suited driver/one black-suited security) at the bank, 8 a.m. 1 p.m.—same cast—driven to a modern box of a luxury apartment building. Each unit set behind a garish yellow concrete pad like slices of butter on an upended plate. 2 p.m., the banker's car emerged from underground parking. Add a twenty-something model-type to the driver/security combo, who cuddled into the curve of Abbatantuono's neck—

Definitely post-coital, but the dude's on a clock.

—2:15 p.m. Starbucks (same one, three in a row) near a walking street of high-end shopping. The girl would walk one way with a fist of cash; Abbatantuono, back to his Audi limousine. Back to bank headquarters until 6 p.m., when he'd head out to dinner, meet same young doll who would gleefully introduce him to the contents of all her shopping bags, followed by an Audi limo dash at 8:35/8:05/9:17 p.m. (respectively) to the Four Seasons Hotel des Burges. He would escort his girlfriend inside and—ever the quick-shot artist—would be out alone in time to be home between 10:30 and 10:45 p.m. Lights would go out at the Abbatantuono villa precisely at 11 o'clock.

It would have been easier, Michael supposed, if Kalaydoskop had poked his head round a corner and photobombed his surveillance as he had in the Father Cevik photos. Then, Michael would have simply made a run at the old communist. He could wait. Build a better profile/plan. But Michael hadn't missed the WaPo story of his asset/"al Qaeda drug courier" gunned down in his Christmas jacket at Dulles. Remembered Father Cevik executed in a Turkish dungeon. His truck ride up into the Turkish mountains with a shovel to dig his own grave. No. People wanted Michael dead, and since he didn't know who'd ordered it or why, it was better to make his move on Abbatantuono ASAP. His own survival would not wait.

Lynn would rendition the guy. Hal would drop him. Me...shucks, I'm a people person. Who's to say he won't like me once we meet?

Michael's humor vanished.

Must have liked my mom. At some point.

How much better it would have been for everyone had Michael taken more time? But until Michael knew the piece of beach glass Antonio Abbatantuono added to the kaleidoscope, the rules and purpose of both Kalaydoskop and, he would learn, KALEIDOSCOPE, and why it called for people to die—his mother, he suspected, not least of all—Michael had to use his best resources immediately at hand.

♔♔♔

Like Michael, Mrs. Helene Favre was also a people person. It was Helene who provided Michael the intelligence necessary to enact his meet-and-greet. One glimpse of the girlfriend whose picture Michael had caught with his phone elicited a peal of laughter.

"Come on, private-eye," she teased. "Everyone knows small-'e'-accent, super-model, and never-be-but-wannabe pop sensation—" a dramatic pause, mocking her dramatic pronouncement: "échappé."

"*Gesundheit*? What's a small-'e'-accent e-frappe?"

"*échappé* is a ballet term. It literally means *'to escape.'*" More dra-mockery. "But she uses it as a single name identity. Like Iman."

"She'd probably look pretty good doing ballet—I'll give her that."

Helene met his eyes in her sewing table mirror. Stern.

"You would be wrong. No one will say it publicly, but she is a terrible dancer. They say she can't even twerk."

"What's that?"

"I have no idea, but they say that in her ill-fated music video, she attempted the twerk and looked as if she were fighting constipation."

"You say 'no one will say it,' but you seem to know a lot of what people are saying."

"She's the reason Madame Abbatantuono filed for divorce but refuses to move out or make any move on it. It's a dog fight. But three dogs. Monsieur Abbatantuono the most rabid."

Michael crossed his arms. Gave stern right back. "How come you know all this stuff? And I still can't find anything."

"Because as Swiss, we do not engage in public gossip."

Michael sneered. "Where do you engage in it."

Helene straightened her black dress and went to Michael's internet terminal. She signed in to her Facebook groups and Twitter account.

Three days of surveillance/three nights internet gossip. This is what Michael learned:

Madame Abbatantuono, originally Lily Huber, had been a 1960s European film star. Antonio Abbatantuono stole her heart and denied Lily her career. She became *Il Fiore Appassito di Villa Abatantuono* The Wilted Flower of Villa Abbatantuono. She put up with her husband's numerous affairs with budding starlets and models whose careers he seemed to ruin as well as he'd ruined hers. And there was always hope for a comeback. In 2010, talk swirled about a role for Lily Huber in a Roman Polanski film the director never made. This disappointment, coupled with her husband's sudden financing of small-'e'-accent échappé's singing career, was all too much. Lily Huber-Abbatantuono filed for divorce.

Now she lived as his prisoner, allowing the case to stall in fear that if she proceeded, she would wind up with nothing. Ten-month stalemate. People suspected two things: Lily Huber was bluffing and desperate to win Antonio back, and échappé—knowing this and feeling she might lose her sugar daddy, demanded he get the divorce and marry her. There were those who thought that, even with a lowercase-'e'-accent, échappé had the upper hand. Lily Huber-Abbatantuono had been barren all these years; échappé would bear him a son. And boy, did she like to fuck.

By mid-afternoon—while Antonio and échappé enjoyed their Starbucks, Michael bought the most inexpensive diamond engagement ring he could purchase from the trendiest jeweler he could find. He sent word to Madame Huber-Abbatantuono—through her long-suffering publicist's office—saying he'd just sold said ring to her husband after small-'e'-accent échappé tried it on. He suggested they speak immediately and left the number of Mrs. Favre's shop. At the appointed hour—about the time Antonio and échappé were getting it on at the Four Seasons (though maybe he'd already finished), Helene answered the telephone as jewelry store receptionist and transferred the call to Michael by handing him the receiver.

Michael greeted Mrs. Huber-Abbatantuono. Asked if she didn't mind speaking in English.

In English, she expressed her confusion and insult that he would reach out to her in any language. "I will not be stalked or tormented!"

"Madame, I would be eternally ashamed were I to do either."

"Or toyed with."

"This is no such game."

Helene rolled her eyes. Michael shrugged. Madame Huber-Abbatantuono didn't hang up. After a moment, she observed, "You are American. You do not work in a Swiss jewelry shop."

"The ring and the circumstances *are* authentic, but no. The person I've been stalking is your rotten husband."

"Enough. I'm calling the police."

She didn't hang up.

"If you feel that's right. All I wanted to do was give you what you need to ensure a settlement before I ruin him."

The former Lily Huber (acting now) laughed. "You are insane. Good bye."

She didn't hang up.

Michael said, *"Le sex-appeal torride de Kim Novak avec un flair dramatique plus grand que celui d'Anne Bancroft et Patricia Neal réunis."*

Helene applauded, making sure her hands did not touch. She'd worked with him on that—*The steamy sex appeal of Kim Novak with a dramatic flair greater than Anne Bancroft and Patricia Neal combined.*

"What did you just say?"

Michael: "'No sea could be as cold as your heart of stone—Baby!'" A one-two punch of her most important review, followed by her most famous line. He imagined he could feel the flutter of her heart across the wires.

Silence. Small— "I was, you know, all that."

"Antonio Abbatantuono stole the brightest star from the heavens when he denied you your career."

A sniffle. "What do you want from me?"

"Think of me as your shining knight. I want to rescue you and set you free."

Helene dropped her jaw and finger-pointed the universal "vomit" sign.

Michael poured it on thicker. "I have information that your husband will pay a fortune for."

"Blackmail?"

"I prefer business intelligence." He paused. This was the clincher. "Kalaydoskop; have you heard of it?"

"I know nothing of my husband's business."

"No one knows much about Kalaydoskop and that's what makes it so valuable. I want to meet you. Give you what I have for safekeeping. I will then arrange a meeting with him. He will pay me. I will give you half, and you will give him the document in exchange—predicated he signs your divorce settlement to whatever terms you've dictated."

They agreed to meet at eleven the next morning. Michael gave her the name of a hotel, told her the room number and name to ask for. The desk would give her a key. He praised her talent, lamented her lost career, suggested she would give the world a gift when, soon free, she might take to the silver screen again. They said goodbye.

Helene said, "You understand, she'll never show."

Michael said, "Stranger things have happened," and that was what he counted on. He asked if he could borrow a customer's black suit jacket from Helene's alterations rack.

"Get any of your foolish blood on it—you buy the whole suit."

Michael took the diamond ring from its velvet box. He closed it in her hand. "Collateral."

She smiled, but she was dreadfully worried; neither of them had considered how deeply and stupidly Michael had involved her when he'd scooted aside and let her sign him in to her social media accounts.

2.

T HERE ARE AS FEW comic moments in a case officer's career as there are in Malory's telling of *The Death of Arthur.* One incident, though, told not only by Malory but by his modern translator, John Steinbeck, and other Arthurian authors, is how Lancelot gets tricked out of his armor by a damsel and climbs naked up a tree to fetch her hunting hawk, only to have her husband appear below, fully armed and armored, to challenge the naked Round Table knight to a fight to the death. The version told by T.H. White in Doris Kingston's favorite book and read to Michael's childhood glee at her dining room table round table, was much on Michael's mind the next morning when he arrived at the hotel to meet the Wilted Flower of Villa Abbatantuono, Madame Huber-Abbatantuono.

Half an hour before eleven, Antonio Abbatantuono's 20-foot, six-door, gray Audi limousine pulled to the curb around the corner from the entrance to the small boutique hotel where Michael had taken a room. Abbatantuono/driver/two security. Before leaving the vehicle, the security men twisted silencers into the muzzles of their two automatic handguns. Left the car. Stalked around the corner. Entered the hotel. Within five minutes, called back to Abbatantuono's driver to report that the blackmailer had not arrived.

Abbatantuono: *"Nous attendons."* We wait.

Five more minutes.

Abbatantuono barked at his driver. *"Je n'aime pas. Soyez vigilant."* I don't like it. Make yourself vigilant.

The driver got out. Walked around to the curb. Slowly scanned. All directions. He saw her rushing the limousine before Abbatantuono heard échappé's (small-'e'-accent) excited squeal.

"Mon amour! Mon merveilleux, beau, viril, homme-tigre! Où est-il! Oui je le veux" My love! My wonderful, handsome, virile, man-tiger! Where is it? Yes, I want it! The size of her perfect smile accentuated the size of gleaming white and perfect teeth. She bent lower and lower, as her heel stacatto'd the pavement, her perfect hand holding out the open and empty velvet box. *"Ma bague! Notre bague de fiançailles ! Tu l'as fait, mon trésor!"* My ring! Our engagement ring! You've done it, my treasure!

Antonio Abbatantuono stared at his bimbo with a kind of horror. *"Sortez-la d'ici!"* Get her out of here!

The driver grabbed the girl. She struggled. He bear-hugged her. She struggled. Confusion, anger—a whispered word—and fear. She struggled less, and he marched her forcefully down the sidewalk. Moments passed. Abbatantuono barely relaxed as the driver slid back behind the wheel. Shut/locked the doors. Ab-batantuono fiddled with his phone. Barked, *"Fais-moi sortir d'ici!"* Get me out of here!

Not understanding the words, the black-jacketed dri-ver already had the transmission engaged and was flooring the accelerator when he took the time to hold up the driver's pistol and say, "Give me the phone. Do anything other than sit tight—I'll kill you."

Abbatantuono did as Michael requested. Michael shut off the phone. Abbatantuono seemed to relax. "You know they will kill you."

He's not talking about his security.

Michael sped toward highway A1A out of the city. For a few minutes, neither man spoke. As Michael merged into traffic, he tossed a fragment he'd saved from the Cevik photos into the backseat. "It's my only one. Don't crease it."

Abbatantuono looked at the cut-out image of Kalaydoskop beneath the Pell and Glatisant logo.

Michael said, "You recognize that man?"

Abbatantuono shook his head. "No." He offered it back.

"I was afraid you were going to say that."

"You know nothing about Kaleidoscope—nothing more than a name."

Michael said nothing.

"The less you do know, the luckier for you. Since going any further will get us both killed. We can save each other's lives by letting each other go."

Michael found the exit he was looking for. Outskirts. A road meandering through farmland.

The silver-haired banker pressed. "It would only risk my life if I pursued you after this. It is a system, a force, unforgiving, and much more powerful than either of us can handle. We would be safe from one another in our mutually assured destruction."

Michael drove through the center of the neighborhood. Past the commuter train station. Said, "Isn't this the point where you offer me money?"

Abbatantuono chuckled. "This isn't blackmail or a kidnapping." His eyes met Michael's gaze in the rearview. "I see something entirely different. It's in your face. Not unfamiliar. You're as foolish as she—playing with matches."

Michael found the lane he sought. It dead-ended between the far end of a farm field and the tree-lined backside of the Promenade de l'Aire ecological park. U-turned. Faced out. Backed into leafy shadows.

"Killing me would be a fatal mistake." Abbatantuono.

"I perfectly understand how you'd see it that way." Michael.

Michael got out of the car. Went around. Opened Abbatantuono's door. Waved the pistol. "Let's get this done."

Abbatantuono braced where he sat. Michael shoved the pistol into his waistband. Grabbed the silver-haired banker's lapels. "Out." Sent him sprawling in the grass. "Get up." When Abbatantuono didn't: "Geez, if I was going to kill you, don't you think I'd have done it in the car?" Let it sink in. Reinforced, "I don't kill people."

"Where's my driver? You have his gun."

"I bumped his head into a wall. I'm sure he's fine. Get up. Have some dignity."

Abbatantouno reluctantly pushed himself to his feet. "What now?"

"You give me Kaleidoscope, I let you go."

Dumbfounded, Abbatantuono laughed. "You think I'd bring anything with me? Those account books are locked up inside my vault."

"I believe the originals are, but here's what I'm thinking—"

"You really are a fool."

"Maybe. But here's the thing: I think it's so big and my threat so odd and wildly foolish—as I'm sure you got every detail from your wife—that it got you scared."

Abbatantuono's laughter died out. Still, he grinned.

Michael winked. "A bit. Just enough—and I'm betting I'm right—that the clever part of you wondered if the invitation to the hotel might be a ruse to keep you away from an assault on your bank."

Abbatantuono's grin died too.

"Yep. I saw the army you deployed there. Bankers are cautious by nature. Cover every angle. Every contingency. So, a part of you had to worry—what if, somehow/some way, that assault proved successful? You'd need some digital copy and a way to move it all. Make the originals redundant. Fast."

"You tire me."

"History's on my side on this. Frightened kings and thieves traveled with their treasure. King John—frightened by war—flees the safety of his castle only to bumble across a river and watch his crown jewels swallowed up by quicksand and whirlpools. Why no pirate map ever yielded any gold beneath an 'X.' It's always found where they went down with their ship."

Abbatantuono swept his hand at his limo. "Search the ship."

Michael spread his open palms in a gesture of—"Thank you. We'll start with you. Empty your pockets."

Off came the banker's suit jacket. He emptied the pockets onto the limo's hood. He waited for Michael to at least go through his wallet, but Michael didn't touch a thing. Abbatantuono shrugged. Folded his jacket. Placed it on the hood. Emptied his pants pockets. Michael didn't move. Antonio Abbatantuono took off his shoes. Shook them. Showed them empty to Michael. Michael didn't take them. A shoe dangling from each hand, he held out his arms away from his body. "Seach me?"

"No need. You already showed me where it is."

Michael lifted the suit jacket. Abbatantuono's face drained of color. A quick pat down produced a thumb drive.

"Don't take it so hard. From the minute your wife didn't hang up on me, it was always going to end this way."

Michael used the jacket to sweep the rest of the junk from the Audi's hood. He walked around. Slid in behind the wheel. A second thought. A dart back around. He grabbed Abbatantuono's shoes. "I'll leave them and the jacket in the car."

The silver-haired old man dogged Michael around to the driver's side. Crowded him. Michael aimed the gun. Abbatantuono didn't believe he'd use it and tried to push his way inside. Michael shoved him hard on his ass.

"It's encrypted! The money will all be gone by the time you open those files."

"I hope you all choke on it." Michael slammed the door. Locked the vehicle. Lowered his window as he put the car into drive. "Listen: that mutual destruction assurance? You make a move against me, what's happened here—" he wagged the storage device. "It'll blow back on you."

He told Abbatantuono where he could claim his vehicle, and drove off. By the time—silk socks shredded—the old banker reached the local commuter station, though long gone—

Lynn would have squeezed him; Hal would have killed him.

—Michael had been true to his word.

THAT NIGHT, Antonio Abbatantuono, President and CEO of Pell & Glatisant Trading Conglomerate, GmbH did something remarkable. He fucked his girlfriend, small-'e'-accent échappé *and* made love to his wife. First time in ten years. With each, he forced himself to last long enough that he had the satisfaction of knowing he'd left them satisfied. He went into his wine cellar. Uncorked a 1982 Chateau Lafite Rothschild. A vintage as remarkable as his night. He didn't bother to decant it. Quaffed half the bottle in one go from the neck.

When you have every possible thing a human being can want—could replicate it one thousand times, could have it all a thousand different ways—but your soul is empty, love is dull. Happiness is flat and meaningless. Pleasure becomes monotonous and meaningless; a repetitive, singular chemical sensation. What you have, what you thrive on, is power. From power, respect.

From respect, dignity. From dignity, supreme faith in yourself, which is inseparable from your realm.

Avoir été humiliée d'abord par elle, puis par son fils. Bêtement. Facilement. To have been humiliated first by her, then by her son. Foolishly. Easily. He smashed the bottle. He shredded his wrists. His blood mixed with the wine. He thought, *They would make it look like suicide, so what's the difference?* At least the part of his life named death, would not be a lie.

3.

*S*HARING *I*S *C*ARING – *Gently Loved Kids' Clothes.* Between the *Smile Bright* laser dentistry and a luxury residential real estate and escrow, both high-end services, Melody didn't think the children's resale store, opened in March, stood much of a chance for success. When Melody shopped for the twins, she always stopped here first. Outside, after successful purchases of bathing suits for the twins and outfits they didn't hate for Paige's birthday dinner, she froze.

"I lost my Crocs." Little Silas. He lifted one of his bare feet for his mother to see.

"How?" All she could get out. Sounded dumb. Couldn't focus. Embarrassment.

Jack. "He took them off when you tried on the bathing suit." His eyes danced between the two.

Melody stared at the foot. Any moment, the real estate office door would open.

The boys shared a curious look.

"Mom, we'll go back and get 'em." Little Silas. "I remember where they are."

His foot looks like my foot, and my feet are hers.

HER FATHER'S stretched-out white tube sock. Its tip stuck under the leg of their second-hand kitchen table. Mama's foot pulled from it in falling. She lies backwards from the table and, shot perfectly through the heart, she is already dead.

It replays slower than slow motion. Still frames; the hearts of moments. Isolated and held in place. It is the sounds that live. And repeat—and the terror and the horror—and never die.

Mama glows joy. Grips her chairback. Behind it. Loose pages of a contract mess the tiny table.

"It's a statewide chain, but they're going national. The dresses to start, but some of the blouses and the slacks. That's my name—Roberta—and our shared name, Kel-so—"

The first slap. Her head snapped profile. She pretends it didn't happen. "I'll hire seamstresses—"

Pretends she doesn't feel it, but I see a hundred tiny dots of blood.

"We'll get a bigger place—"

The second slap. Same side. His reach incredibly long.

She makes the sound of a wounded animal; I see the other side of her face unnaturally fitting the edge of the doorframe she has slammed against.

I wail. She murmurs—trying to sound sweet—guttural: "It's okay, Melody. Go into the bedroom. Shut the door. Boone-y, you won't have to stress between commissions."

"Stupid bitch. You just don't get it."

I don't move. She is back. Hunched. Hanging onto her chairback. Pink drool-string hangs from her lips. She looks down. Her eyes are wide. I can see the whites.

"You can stop drinking your poison—you call it that—and be creative, and paint—"

Her hand. Fingers crooked. Tips caress his cheek.

"And you can spread your legs for more strangers the minute I'm gone?"

Weak: "Boone Kelso, you know that isn't true."

Bone snapping. Mama howling.

Mama's wrist hanging wrong. Her other fist swings at his face. Wide. She is screaming.

And he's been sitting all this time. And then he's not. I see his pistol in the back of his pants.

I'm screaming.

Her tight-coiled curls between his fingers; her broken, bloody face, eyes askew after the third time he pounds it into the tabletop. Mama staggers back. Daddy grabs the front of her dress. She wrenches back, and it tears, and her breasts flop, and I flash that we're all just animals. God's pitiful creatures.

Loud in my mind: I'll kill you! I lunge for him. I'll kill you! My blood so hot, my rage so fat inside me. My voice doesn't work.

But I hold the gun.

"Give me the gun, Mel."

Sight and sound tumble all together, like slipping on ice too fast, unstoppable. His snatching hands. My scuttling back. Mama convulsing but somehow pulling herself back to where she started out so joyfully, hands lumped on the back of her chair.

"I'll kill you!" It comes out now, so loud that I never hear the gunshot when I pull the trigger. Daddy's eyes wide. Head-whip. He watches with me: Mama slams backwards into the sink and drops.

I am ten years old.

Daddy says, "You saved me, Mel. You saved us both."

The sole of Mama's foot is the color of the top of my foot. The top of her foot is the color of my eyes.

Except for the blood.

♛ ♛ ♛

"DON'T YOU look like someone just stepped on your grave? Girl, what are you doing here?"

Melody's gaze shifted outward. Gwen. The man who had kissed her cheek goodbye—

I'm cool with that.

But copped a feel of her breasts—

And she'd leaned into it. Uncool beyond belief; I know what I saw.

Through the window behind Gwen, the flouncy, silk-pocket-squared sonofabitch tried to look all up-an-up; gave Melody a little wave, and Gwen noticed, and Gwen said, "Oh. Nelson. Handsy. Kind of a douche. Big contract, though. Michael was thrilled when I told him," and Melody—

Just glad the boys missed that.

—pursed-lip smiled, kind of, and nodded like a bobblehead.

Nelson Fair was about to step out and join them to shove it in Melody's face, but Gwen said, "Sister talk,

Nelly. I promise. You and I will christen the new listing tomorrow. Girl Scout's honor." She poised her fingers in the Boy Scouts salute, then used them to shove him back indoors. Up-downed Melody with her eyes. "Hi."

"Hi."

"Why are you here?"

To spit in your eye.

Melody blinked. Begged her smile to remain on her face.

Jack and Little Silas blasted out of the resale kids' store with a chorus of "Found 'em! We found 'em! Hiya, Aunt Gwen!"

Melody lifted her recycled grocery bag that contained the clothing. "Picking up a few things."

Gwen wrinkled her nose. "How nice."

"We're excited for Paige's big night. Aren't we, guys?"

They grinned, staring now.

I wish they wouldn't do that. At least we don't shop at "Hotties" like she does; I can't scold them in front of her.

Patience.

Michael.

She's looking into the void.

Melody said, "I thought it *really* nice she's choosing dinner with the family."

"There'll be a couple of friends. We need to make sure we have enough. She's going out tonight. Big eighteen moment at midnight or whatever." Gwen roughed both boys' hair. "They grow up so fast. Treasure you have so much leisure time with them." She smiled at Melody.

Melody summoned the other ghost from the other trinity that truly/purely/gracefully defined her life. Summoned kindness. Smiled truly/purely/gracefully back.

Gwen said, "Showings to check up on. Never stops." Waved. Stepped off.

"Bye, Aunt Gwen!"

They're six, they don't even know why they're looking.

But the ghosts weren't through with her, and Melody heard herself call, "He's missing, Gwen! Not dead!"

Gwen beeped her way into the car. Leaned out. Toodle loo'd Jack and Little Silas with a roll of her lacquered fingers. "Not according to your husband. See you all back at the Farm."

♕ ♕ ♕

"I AM SO SORRY to bother you, Mrs. Jenkins. You are headed to Foxtail Farm, I believe?"

George Washington University Hospital night nurse Janella Jenkins came down her front steps wheeling her suitcase, her medical bag propped on top.

"Who're you?"

"A man who eats, drinks, works, plays, prays, and cusses all too much, which makes me a Texan."

Janella cocked her head at the stout man in the damp, yellowing linen suit.

"We're a long way from the ice cream booth at the county fair, and you know where I'm going, so you know I'm late." She wheeled the concrete path to the driveway and her sunburned Subaru. "Now, unless you po-lice, you quit dripping sweat all over my car and let me be."

She moved at ramming speed. He hopped aside, light-footed for a heavy man, especially considering he tipped an imaginary hat.

"Not police. No, no, not law enforcement at all. I promise you: no one is in any kind of trouble. But—" and he drew out the coordinating conjunction for about this long, followed by— "I'm also 'worried.' Which makes me from the government." And Morton Drexler proved it by flashing his credential.

Janella Jenkins widened her eyes with open skepticism, if not hostility.

"Ma'am, while you are looking after Ms. Kingston's health, her coworkers must continue looking after the health of the nation—all without bringing her any undue stress."

The nurse's expression didn't change.

"While in the hospital, her communications—balanced against the drugs administered that may, *or may not*, one never knows, affect her clear-headedness—were easy for us to monitor and protect. But, what-with her being in a private home..."

Her shoulders relaxed. Her features relaxed. Morton Drexler knew the rest would be easy.

4.

*J*UNCTION *32*. IF YOU don't remember—and if you are under the age of twenty-eight, memory would be impossible for what had once been, had vanished before you were born—observing the road sign, green background/reflective white lettering, with an additional, sun-blistered orange decal/black lettered *No Outlet* over the exit arrow. You would barely register the off-ramp and would motor past to anything else that offered even a little something more than this, which the sign allowed/claimed/warned offered nothing. That would be at normal (which was usually high speed, this stretch of Maryland 5 below 235/Prince Frederick Road), but slow enough, say, the rare construction zone/less rare traffic accident ahead. With the sun hitting the sign just right, you might glimpse the darker green silhouette of the former name. Not completely covered by the new off-putting off-ramp *Junction 32*, are two words whose anticipation, first sight, mere thought, mention, shriek or cry, once inspired and delighted, entertained and sparked by thousands, the candle flame of imagination, hope and dreams of a wondrous place of childhood gloriosity. Two words. *Enchanted Forest.*

"Slow down, you'll miss it. There it is—Junction 32."

Clive swerved onto the exit ramp. Paige squeezed his thigh. "You did it. We're here."

"Here's where? It's pitch-dark. I'm going to run into a bog."

"You won't. Trust me. It's here, up ahead. But it's a-ways. My dad says cars used to line up an hour back on the highway."

Clive's headlights illuminated six all but faded lanes once plied by in/out-going traffic, now cracked and pot-holed, and piled by weeds. The road bent into the prevailing woods and, further ahead, was the hulk of one last ruined parking lot kiosk.

"No need to get out your wallet. Parking's free. I'm a cheap date."

The blacktop that covered the large parking lot beyond the kiosk had broken, crumbled, vanished. Two-thirds of it swelled with mounds of junk, garbage, the unsalvageable material of an aborted park demolition. Border privet and river kudzu tangled most of it.

Clive drove toward the glow of headlights. The thump of music. The shrill of voices, laughter, song. Some leftover bottle rockets went up and popped over the crooked metal entry arch—gates long stripped away. Large, worked iron letters headed the arch. *Enchanted Forest.* Beneath and re-hung unevenly with both original and commercial chain, drooped the original wooden placard: *Merlyn and Morgana Bid You Welcome!*

"I bet your friend likes that."

"Whenever some dude gets the hots for her, she tells them to climb up and get rid of the last 'A.'"

Clive stared up at it. "Still there."

Paige smirked. "Yeah. They always get their asses kicked by everyone else, who're *never* gonna let it change."

Walking now. Past mostly younger kids—fourteen to sixteen years-old—partying, dancing in the beds of trucks and between cars and a few portable charcoal grills. No kegs. A lot of cans—mostly energy drinks, from what Clive could see. Someone powered a rack of twirling dance lights from a car battery. Paige explained, you didn't get allowed inside until you were seventeen, and maybe not always then.

"Everyone cooperates?"

"Tradition. Been this way forever."

What about the authorities?"

"You can add two and two? Do the math."

Took a sec. Winked. "The underage ones are lookouts. For the older ones inside. Kids can't get into that much trouble."

"You're cute when you're smart." Paige clutched his arm as they passed through to the gate. "I started coming here when I was fifteen. Maybe one hundred times. I've seen cops all of twice. An ambulance, once, when a kid once got bit by a copperhead. I dunno—maybe the cops' kids come here. Maybe *they* came here."

"This been going on that long?"

"Since the place was abandoned."

Beyond the gate was a cluster of ruined shops and booths; what had once been a fanciful medieval village, conquered, plundered, and deserted. At the far end of the overgrown lane that ran perpendicular from the shambled hamlet, a dark and crumbling castle with two dilapidated towers loomed, shedding beams and chicken wire stucco, at once scowling and minacious and inviting as moonlight has always drawn humans with its silver cloak of fancied magic.

"They say this whole place shut down because two little kids went inside the castle—cotton-candy-happy as can be—and were never seen again. Not even on security camera video."

"OOOoooo..." Clive made a spooky sound. Paige punched his arm. All at once and all around them, lighters and matches flared. Ignited sparklers and brilliant fountains and colorful smoke bombs to cries of "Paige! Paige! Paige!" and "Woot-woot!" shouts, applause and whistles and yells. "Happy Birthday!"

Clive heard Paige catch her breath in one sharp gasp. She hugged him, arms wound round his waist. He looked down into her glowing face. She beamed, radiant.

Morgan—over-dressed, but equally perfect to the moment—stepped out in front of them, silver sequins dazzling her short little dress.

"Happy B-day, Bestie."

Paige peeled from Clive. Squealing, the two girls collided, their hands gripping each other's shoulders.

Some dude put a beer in Clive's fist. "Lucky man, bro. She's da bomb."

"Thanks, bruv. Don't I know it."

And I can't think of any way out of being the one who's going to ruin it and hurt her more than anyone should ever have the right.

Paige looked back at him. Beckoned him to come properly meet her very best friend in the world.

This is such fucking bullshit what you're going to do! She's just—

Her grinning eyes glistened. He couldn't remember ever seeing anyone so aboundingly happy.

Loveliness. Pure, simple loveliness. You can't do this, Clive. Not to her.

But he had no way out of it. "Cheers," he said. "You must be Morgan."

FIRES WERE SHUNNED—candles, sometimes, when people paired off and went somewhere to get romantic—but never bonfires or brazier-type fire pits you get from Home Depot. All the groups that partied in the Enchanted Forest policed themselves and each other. Some would bring battery lanterns; most preferred the natural light of the moon and how, when darkness brought everything closer, it made the mystical world around them feel elsewhere and larger. Music, dancing, drinking, gossiping and analyzing life and making out with boyfriends—that's about all that went on with Paige's crew. Some kids smoked. Cigarettes, mainly. Or boys stealing their fathers' cigars. But some were into pot and no one really cared, and, even if there was blow going around, or other rave drugs like Molly, people kept that on the down low. Of course, there were always the trippers out wandering around or howling at the moon with their acid or mushrooms and their Queens of the Stone Age, and Radiohead, and the Grateful Dead, who it seemed would never die. But for Paige's crowd, there was mostly pop music and dancing and drinking games. Morgan had picked out the old princess carousel and the cement pad next to it that had been the Merlin's Kitchen dining area that still had the twenty-foot stone-sculpted, green-eyed owl.

Paige sat on a concrete rail fence made to look like creeping vines, now host to the real thing. Clive perched next to her. They shared champagne from a plastic cup and watched Paige's friends and the accumulated strangers splash beer and cocktails as they danced to someone's playlist.

"It's all such a ritual. All this. Every weekend, every party," said Paige.

"You're not having fun?"

"I couldn't be having more fun. Are *you* having fun?"

"What do you mean, ritual? Like religion?"

She gave him a sidelong glance. "Like a religion, yeah-maybe, a religion focused entirely on the sensation of now."

She hopped off the rail. Offered her hand. He took it.

I can't believe this is going to happen. Be cool...

Clive said, "Sometimes the now is enough."

"If you keep your now filled to overflowing, then the eternal doesn't have room to come into play."

"Ah. The afterlife."

"More like infinity—the eternal without before and after but encompassing everything all at once."

She was leading him deeper into the old amusement park. "You know, my dad—aunt and uncle—even my grandmother had birthdays here."

He's enjoying being led...

Clive kissed her. She kissed him back. They continued their walk.

"You always like this? So philosophical about...party-ing?"

"It's why I always end up on the edge of the party." The ground beneath her feet squished. "There's this wooden planks and crate stuff. We gotta find it because it gets kinda wet in here. People always lose their shoes. Here it is." She led him onto the makeshift wooden path.

"Really. Or are you just trying to impress me because you're an adult now and I'm older?"

I am an adult. He's telling me he knows it's about to happen where we're going.

God! Paige! Stop analyzing. (Being with him feels just so perfect, so right.) Be cool.

"If you're trying to come off older, don't get soooo into beer pong."

The marshy patch ran through the center of a lane of children's attractions—Ali Baba's Magic Cave, Jack's Climbing Beanstalk, the Three Bears Cottage. They stopped at a mostly disintegrated Jolly Roger Pirate Ship.

"It's bloody bonkers, this place. That they'd just leave it like this."

"I told you. It's cursed. Those two kids."

"That's not real, is it?"

Paige laughed. "I don't know. But the guy who owned it—he just shut it down. They started to dismantle it, but he stopped them."

They kissed some more. Lust warmed between them.

He's following my lead completely. Don't blow it. (God, I want him more than anything.)

Her happiness overcame her. She laughed and pulled back.

"What?" He was enjoying her.

"Tell you what—I can show you two ghosts. But it's not my fault if you lose your shoes."

She took his hand and led him off the path and as they moved around the derelict ship, a lagoon revealed itself, wide and sparkling with starlight. "This was the Lady in the Lake Lagoon. My dad said this woman would rise with King Arthur's sword and there would be a fountain show. But this way—" She veered off toward a dark screen of wild trees. "It used to be grass, but like three years ago, we had this part of a hurricane that blew over, and Indian Creek overflowed. But here it is. Check this out—" and she spread open a screen of creepers.

"Blow me!"

"What?!"

"You know—holy crap—like what are we looking at?"

Once it had been the mechanical jousting attraction. But mired now in swamp, the broken down steeds barely came above the surface with their metal skeleton-frame heads, making the more-than-scarecrow/less-than-human knights tangled in plastic trash and brambles appear like gleaming wraiths in eternal battle.

"They were like robots—" she clenched tightly to him, speaking between kisses— "on these mechanical horses that would somehow fight." She pulled his hand to her breasts. He didn't resist. He kissed her neck and down her throat, and her words came breathlessly: "I don't know how it worked." She reached low. "But—" Between his legs. "Behind them, up through those trees—" She felt him growing; his fingers beneath her blouse—"That old building. The King's Pavillion. Morgan set it up for us."

His hands stopped. She met his eyes. She could see the depth of his feelings for her, his desire, but there was something else.

"What?"

He kissed her lips.

"We can't do this."

"You don't like it? You don't want to? We can go back to your place—"

What's going on? Stop talking. Shut up.

"I think you're perfectly marvelous. And I want you. And it would be real—"

"Oh. No."

He quickly kissed her. Put a finger to her lips and shook his head.

"It isn't that! It's not pretend. Don't think it—I know what you're thinking—it's not *that.* I want you more than I ever knew was possible to want a woman, but..."

Her eyes glistened. "You have somebody."

"Oh, Paige... Paige... Paige... There's *only* you." He held her. And she heard sorrow in his voice as he kept whispering her name. She didn't know why.

"It's real for me too, Clive. We can wait."

His voice caught in his throat. He said, "Yeah." Because he knew. She couldn't do the math.

Sunday, July Eleventh – Paige's Birthday

1.

Hal burned through his first MasterCard in two stops on his route to the Parc le Grange. Sporting goods super store. Hunting apparel. Forest green wool cap. Woodland pattern light anorak. Camo pattern day pack. Shooting gloves. Tempted by an excellent selection of tactical knives, he walked past. Didn't want to get pro-filed. Coop Supermarket. Pack of underwear. Pack of black tees. Toothpaste/toothbrush. Water bottle. Basic first aid kit. Box of protein bars. Box of electrolyte/mul-tivitamin mix packets. School chalk. Splurged on a ready-made sandwich he ate hoofing it to a hardware store where he lucked out finding a military-grade mul-ti-tool among their knife selection. That burned most of his second card, but what Lynn hadn't considered, and Hal hadn't felt the need to remind her, was he'd be on overwatch. Eyes on a trash bin/dead drop. Not cozied up in a feather bed.

Entered the park. Hal filled his water bottle at the facilities near the main entrance. Took his time to ob-serve the other visitors coming and going around him. Ran an easy SDR establishing that neither he nor his target coordinates were under surveillance. The third time passed, he made his approach.

Strapped to a post, the trash bin stood at the apex of the park's most tightly curved walking path. Below—broad grass sloped one hundred yards, give or take, to an outdoor concert shell. Above—about one hundred feet—a fat copse of trees, thick with hazel under a taller canopy of ash. Hal finished his sandwich. Walked the bag and wrapper to the bin. Less than half-full. Threw them away in pieces long enough to notice two coffee containers. Separate shops. Each with customer name scrawled on its side—*Michel.* He popped the top off both. Only coffee residue. Chalked an X through the name on one and left it beside the post. He continued along the path, down the curve to the next intersection. Took the branch that swung back. Up and around the grove of trees. First opportunity, alone in all directions, he dove into the shrubbery. Made his way through dense foliage. Set up his observation post. Spent the night on watch. Park police rolled through twice. Never stopped. Mosquito-molested through the dead of night; showered by rainbirds with dawn. A gardening/maintenance team came through. Noticed the cup by the post and put it in the bin. Now it would be on top. Drank some enhanced water with a protein bar. Nuts/raisin/chocolate buttons. Waited.

6:00 a.m. The park opened. Visitors trickled by. Serious joggers, followed by the moms with babies, the parents with kids. No one recognizable from the day before. None showed any interest in the dead drop. At 8:18, Hal observed his older brother. Finishing a coffee while he strolled. Walked it to the bin—

Okay, big brother, notice the signal.

—dropped his empty cup inside. Headed off, then stopped. Deliberately turned. All the way around, back the way he came, then back about forty-five degrees. He gazed out that way—as if admiring the amphitheater—checked his wristwatch longer than necessary, then continued forward.

He faced the park's side entrance. Gate he'll leave through. Ten seconds on the wristwatch—the distance he wants me to keep.

Hal slipped from his cover. Hit the dead drop. Grabbed the coffee cup.

Not just coffee this time.

Shoved it in his daypack. Went the direction Michael had come from; circled paths until he reached the exit. Found a bench. Futzed with his phone. Two minutes in place, Michael passed him so close he could have grabbed him. Neither man noticed the other, but ten seconds after Michael left the Parc le Grange, Hal stood up and followed.

THE SIGN ABOVE the door read *Laundrenet.* Michael unlocked the door with a key. Checked his watch, covered a yawn with the back of his hand and disappeared inside.

Yawn. Rest; staying put.

Across and back down the street they'd made their approach, Hal saw an aproned barman setting up tables on the sidewalk outside his bar/café. Hal crossed. Made his way back. Considered taking a seat at a sidewalk table, noticed a better table inside the window. Claimed it. Watched the shop Michael had gone into while the barman brought him a liter of sparkling water and a plate of lemon wedges.

Opening chores and side-work done, the barman split his attention between a sporting newspaper and the ubiquitous European soccer network. Hal reached into his backpack. Into the coffee cup. Pulled out a baggie with a USB flash drive. While he was asking the barman where he could find a mobile phone or electronics store, a singsong voice drifted through the open door.

"Bonjour, American Joe! Ça joue ou bien?" Good morning, American Joe! How's it going?

Hal cringed a little inside. Michael had done everything perfectly, so far, but, to Hal's way of thinking, he always had a problem making friends. He never knew when to stop.

2.

THE FIRST THING JANELLA did the previous evening upon her arrival at Foxtail Farm was tell Lynn about her encounter with Morton Drexler. Actually, that was the second thing. The first thing Janella did was exclaim, "You're on no government salary living in a place like this."

Lynn rolled eyes skyward, texted. *My father's home. Just here to recuperate.*

Stopped between the gravel parking circle and the manor. Janella stepped back, looked up and around, past the manor to the chapel, the North Vista Outhouse, said, "I could get used to recuperating."

Lynn: *Problem is, no one ever gets used to my father.*

"Cueball. I met him."

They shared a grin, and Lynn found Gwen's kids, Melody and hers. Leigh immediately proclaimed that she was going to be a nurse when she grew up, just like Janella, and the twins showed her the portrait painted by Daniel Boone that wasn't but *was* their grandma they'd never met, and Melody helped get Janella situated, and Janella was even *more* impressed when Charlotte corrected her on whose house this was, saying, "Papa *gave* it to Aunt Melody," then embarrassed, quickly added, blushing, "I didn't mean to make that sound like Mom," to which Lynn typed: *"Bitchy,"* by way of explanation; then they were alone and Janella explained what had happened in her driveway.

"I don't know from federal agents, but I'm smart enough to guess his major goal was probably to get me to tell you."

All Lynn offered in return was a small, confirming smirk.

"I need to know, Ms. Kingston. Are you in continued danger from what happened? Am I in danger? This is as nice a place as I have ever walked inside of, but that said, I'm looking to die in my own bed. A great many years from now."

Lynn nodded in understanding. Typed out: *Drexler maybe wasn't wrong in warning you that there are security concerns regarding what happened to me, but I promise—one hundred percent—I was collateral damage. The person who attacked me didn't even know my name.*

Lynn was expert at making a lie dance to the tune of truth. Janella expressed satisfaction with Lynn's response by tending to her unpacking. Stopped suddenly and said, "Why'd they go and build an extra bedroom off a bedroom?"

Lynn was about to tell her it was a night maid's room, when the original maids weren't there by any choice of their own. Typed: *My parents kept separate bedrooms.*

"Wish I could've afforded that when I was married. Sort of like one of them black-and-whites—" caught the way it might have sounded— *"movies.* Just so long as you don't tell me that government man doesn't also take a room here."

Lynn: *Forget about him. He was just warning me to keep my mouth shut.*

"Kinda funny. Considering why I'm here."

In that moment, Lynn knew she'd made the right choice for her health ditching the hospital; she would do anything/everything Janella asked of her for her recovery.

It was now the next morning, and they were on the west porch, which, some time ago, Silas converted into a gym only to realize it was too late into Doris's cancer to be of use or distraction for her, that the grandkids were too young, and that of his children and in-laws only Melody ever thanked him. As Lynn knew, Silas eschewed "cheating" in his own physical fitness— "If I want to run or ride a bike, I'll go outside and actually do it, and there's plenty of work I can do that's A: heavy, and B: gets a job done."

They were discussing the healing process vis-à-vis when Janella would remove the tube and when it would be safe to begin speech— "I have to answer to Dr. Goldfarb at the hospital, and I wouldn't go against anything he said or tells you, but you want to get the best of your speech back? Even after we remove the tube and the valve, you still take two weeks without a peep. You don't want to spend the rest of your life sounding like you'd spent it smoking three packs a day and drinking a quart a'liquor without having had the thrill of the sin."

Honey, you've got no idea.

Lynn was about to make a confession about her drinking—somehow it felt right with Janella—when her burner phone lit up. Incoming data.

♛ ♛ ♛

IT IS DE RIGUEUR in the CIA to manipulate/use/compromise civilians—witting/unwitting, willing and un- —to your mission and its goals. They train you to put the greater good and your higher purpose on a rigged scale of national security, legal sanction, and patriotic duty that you'll use to intellectualize and psychologically justify all negative outcomes (to them, not you) that might arise if things go ass-up. Getting dead, for one. It becomes second nature and, without exaggeration, has saved the world on more than one occasion. The problem with the Kingstons? It was first nature to them. Silas was a clandestine-cannon-fodder master to the point of cruelty. Doris, too—in her civilian time facing the guns—but having learned from the best, and suffered more deeply than anyone, struggled with her three children to dampen this cold tendency in them so that they embraced Christ's second great commandment of "doing unto others..." as spiritually more valuable than lockstep adherence to the vagaries of government designs; she prayed they'd use their power over others as a last resort. By doing so, she atrociously failed the older two of the three.

Like Michael with Helene Favre, Lynn acted with Janella Jenkins R.N., adding deep and heartfelt empathy to the manipulate/use/compromise toolbox. They felt more, thus they damaged more, and one day, someone was going to get killed for it.

After the receipt of the Glatisant digital packet, Hal had switched to the first of his one-time SIMs and texted Lynn a brief update. Lynn instructed Hal to maintain visual contact and support but not to initiate contact. They set a time for their next communication. The files—banking records, Lynn was certain—were encrypted. Possibly easy. Equally, possibly fatal, if she brought them to headquarters, where she was certain specialists could crack it open like a nut. Janella, who had immediately excused herself for coffee, returned as Lynn settled on the next best option.

Lynn typed: *I'm going to need you to take me into the city.*

"I don't take it you're checking back into the hospital."

Lynn explained as little as possible, but it was enough—once Lynn dug up the address—to get a ride in, a drop-off and pickup. It was more than half a long-shot, and there was the specter of Morton Drexler hovering over both their shoulders, but—

If he were actively working a counterintelligence case against me, he wouldn't have come on to Janella and let me know. He's still smarting over Silas pulling the rug out from under him and poking me—via Michael, via Gary, now my in-home care—to see if he can force me to join him.

—so she risked it and paid a call on another Agency retiree, a hard-to-believe former flame of Russell Aiken. An exceptionally clever electronic forensic accountant.

3.

H ELENE FAVRE SAID, "HE must not have liked what you had to say." Worry wrinkled round her steady eyes. "This won't come back here, will it?"

"In the end, that—" he tapped the *Tribune de Genève* she held out to him with its headline announcing the suicide of Abbatantuono— "had absolutely nothing to do with me." Worn out, post-adrenaline crash, Michael didn't inflect the lie convincingly.

"It seems so useless. So sad." She touched the back of his hand. "You seem sad."

"What's the poem? 'Any man's death diminishes me...?'"

"I believe it was a 'Meditation.' You'll be leaving after this?"

"It's my oldest daughter's eighteenth birthday. I'm going to have some dinner and raise a glass of champagne in her honor. I believe, by the time I get to coffee, I'll have an idea of where I'm going."

Helene's worry increased. "I think I'll stay in the harbor. My husband left me a boat. A small sort of barge. Capital-'e'-accent *Échalote*. Ugly, really. I'll feel safer on it there until you're gone. Funny, I kept it this long. But not now, so much. Just right." She touched his face. Goodbye. "I hadn't smiled—hardly left my weaving table—since he died two years ago. Until you came."

"If I don't see you again, thank you. For all your help. I'll leave the key on your table."

She nodded thoughtfully, was about to say something, hesitated, then couldn't help herself. In the cadence of her words, the imagination that lit her eyes, Michael had an instant where he saw her young and lovely and filled with the promise of all the mysteries life had yet to reveal to her. "The photograph of your mother. You didn't know she was here, waiting for you. I saw that in your reaction. But that must mean what you thought drove you here, that drove you after that awful man, and what drove him to take his own life—don't-try-to-sug-ar-coat-it you share responsibility in that—is something entirely different from what you thought."

"In my business, the professional and the personal sometimes collide in strange ways."

"Not the way you expected. I suspected you were per-haps working on behalf of the Americans. But you've left them." Michael nodded. "You are running at something at the same time you are running away from it. Joe."

It's Michael.

"You need to be very careful."

"I always heal," he said.

"Yes. You're strong. Your body is healthy. Your hand-some face is coming right back together. But you quoted the poet."

TO CELEBRATE Paige's birthday, Michael selected an intimate seafood restaurant. Der Seespiegal. Second floor. The outer wall, entirely glass. View of the lake. The fountain with its thematic illuminations. Live jazz. Piano, drums, upright bass. Thematic illuminations on the American songbook. A table for one—though they always have two sides, two seats, and he knew the other would soon fill. He raised his glass of champagne to his daughter. Thought of candles matched to his mother's birthday wishes.

To my Paige: for your intuition. Ever since you were your very smallest, you've seen past lies, misunderstandings and confusion. You embrace the world as it is and why it is without illusion. Keep that and be just.

He felt proud of himself for his sentiment. Awarded himself a smile as he drank the wine. Noticed across the crowded room, in the mirror that backed the bar, his brother Hal subtly toast his beer and bring it to his lips. Glad Hal was there, Michael knew that whomever it was who would show up would not directly pose a threat of danger. Though what he was after—what might be revealed to Michael tonight—wouldn't take his life, he knew he was closer than he'd ever been to losing his soul. To everything that made him who he was as a man, an American, a CIA officer, and a Kingston. He wasn't about to turn back.

Paige's birthday. He hoped she would one day forgive him; it seemed befitting, as tonight would unpack all the birthdays. All the lies, or maybe, having come this far, all the truths.

He was closer tonight to Kalaydoskop than since his first encounter. 1978. Doris's thirtieth birthday. The year of her portrait. The year of the red balloon.

♕ ♕ ♕

LYNN IS THREE—still needs a stroller—but Michael is eight. Thinks himself a "big kid" now. Burgers and French fries. Ice cream and birthday cake in the leafy shade of Merlin's Kitchen beneath the wise, green eyes of the wizard's knowing owl.

Two candles/two wishes—Michael and Lynn; loyalty and faith.

Bards and damsels sing Happy Birthday, *during which Silas disappears.*

Michael explores the Jolly Roger while Doris entertains Lynn watching the water show. The dancing fountains, and rising at their center—

Golden sword. Upstretched arm. The Lady in the Lake.

Silas still missing. Doris says he'll catch up. But Lynn is anxious. The jousting knights and Lynn is frightened.

"He isn't hurt, Linny. They're pretend. The horses are pretend. Lyyyynnn, don't cry over pretend!" Michael dances from foot to foot. He makes funny faces. There is no comforting the girl until Doris offers the carousel.

He comes up out of nowhere. The man. As handsome and magnetic as Michael's own father. He knows their mother. They talk. Doris's throat flushes. Her cheeks. The man gives Michael a red balloon.

Michael holds it aloft. Bounces it in the air at the end of its string. Turns, watching the sun bounce off its bright surface. He sees his father. He has never seen his father look so hurt. So sad. So beaten up. He looks like he's physically shrinking and he's staring, and Michael looks at what Silas is looking at.

The stranger. He is kissing Doris, and Doris is kissing him back. Kalaydoskop's eyes clock Silas. He kisses Doris deeply once more, then ruffles Michael's hair and saunters away. His father does nothing.

♕ ♕ ♕

THE OLDER RUSSIAN man slowly walked to Michael's table. "Is this seat for me?"

"You're not him."

A skeletal man, with the dry, bluish-gray sandpaper skin that comes from decades of cigarette smoke. Mid-fifties, but ancient-appearing, he takes the opposite chair. In Russian-accented English he says, "Any chance you want to share with us what the banker shared with you? I'm Pinwheel."

Michael sat back, insouciant. "Not in a million fucking years. Pinhead. Where's Kalaydoskop?"

Pinwheel smirked. Stifled a cough. Produced a pack of cigarettes. Signaled the waiter for an ashtray. The waiter scowled, but retrieved one from the bar.

"You're not ready to meet him."

"He gets to decide when *I'm* ready?"

"He does. Yes."

The waiter placed the ashtray beside Pinwheel's wrist. Growled, "You have until September."

Pinwheel stopped mid-light. Looked at Michael—*Get a load of this guy*. Michael shrugged.

"The ban begins." The waiter offered. "But most citizens have already adopted it. Will you be having a drink?"

"Your coldest vodka. Russian. No ice."

Pinwheel lit his cigarette. Other customers made a thing of shifting their chairs. Fake coughing. Pinwheel smirked. Said, "There are things he can guide you to discovery, but you must reach your conclusions on your own. Before he will meet you."

"Seems stupid. What's stopping me from taking his help, rolling all this up—including him, you, your whole Soviet-centric crew?"

"We're much older than the Soviets."

"Just like Kaleidoscope is much older than the CIA," he asserted; wasn't denied. "What's to stop me taking you both down?"

Pinwheel chuckled. Choked a little on the tarry edge of the laugh.

Michael: "What's so funny?"

Pinwheel: "He predicted you would say that."

"Did he tell you what answer to give me?"

"Quote: 'If anyone could get away with that, it would be the son of Doris Kingston.'"

Beneath the table, hidden by the tablecloth, Michael dug his fingers into his thighs.

Pinwheel's drink came. With it, the waiter had brought the champagne bottle. Michael nodded him to another glass. Glanced to the bar. Hal was gone. Michael tried not to let that bother him.

Michael said, "Pell and Glatisant isn't your bank—" Pinwheel eyed him over the rim of his tumbler— "as the Cevik photos initially led me to believe."

"You are correct."

"The Cevik photos weren't intelligence on Kalaydoskop. They were from Kalaydoskop."

"Correct again."

"Wasn't it good enough bait for me without having to blow my agent—get him killed? The Turks were tipped off and don't fucking tell me they weren't."

"They were, and that wasn't us."

"You're saying our people—American Kaleidoscope—they did that?"

"We know they killed the colonel."

"The Turkish colonel. The one who kissed me with his boots?"

"Yes. They put him against a wall."

Michael drank. Considered the Russian who considered him back. Glanced to the bar. No Hal. "That doesn't make sense. Kaleidoscope gives the tip on Cevik then assassinates the guy who acts on it?"

Pinwheel lit a fresh cigarette from the end of the one he'd finished. Smashed that one out. "It doesn't make sense. No. One could have been CIA and the other Kaleidoscope—like us, they don't work in cooperation, but then, the one or the other would have taken you in before you ever got to the monastery. It's not how either of us like to work."

"How does it work—in the system?"

"Differently. Outside. We're not intelligence services in the traditional sense. Not at all. We have no interest in political ideologies or military/territorial conquest, subjugation through coercion or brute force. No. That never lasts. Just power-hungry, greedy, angry men's lust for war." He coughed and smoked harder; Michael watched the ash grow. Pinwheel choked into his glass until he could get the rest of his vodka to clear his throat. "This is philosophy, theoretical—not what I'm here to tell you." He twirled his finger in the air to lasso the waiter's attention and another drink. "We are two sides of a single game of chess that was begun by Kaleidoscope, recognized and mirrored by my nation, run on our side by our Kaladoskop. All begun a decade before the Great War and leads toward one victory—world hegemony. It will happen only once—for all the chips, as you say—and in such a way that it will not end the world with war. It will end war as we've known it. It will come as peace, and there will be no rematch, which is why, unlike the game of spies, we have little need to conceal our moves from one another."

"That also seems stupid."

"And yet the kaleidoscope turns, the pieces fall in place." He rose. Put his hand on his cigarette pack. Leaned in. "The best and most effective way to play true chess—a clear winner and clear loser. Each accepting that their fate is not played in darkness, concealing your pieces and your moves. Let the spies playing to narrow, ever-changing agendas do that. This—" he put the cigarette pack in Michael's breast pocket— "is where each opponent can see the other's pieces. Since we're playing a single game for the world, it is better neither side makes mistakes." Pinwheel gave a tight-lipped smile. "Everything. As you get closer, will become clearer."

Michael watched Pinwheel cross the dining room, descend the stairs. Looked to the bar: still no Hal. Michael peeled bills from his wad of cash. Checked the restroom—no Hal. Jogged down the stairs and reached for the front door.

"Not that way." Hal. "They got him soon as he stepped outside. Got another car waiting for you."

"Who?"

"Caucasian. Dressed American. Least he spoke it to your Russian friend."

"No friend of mine."

"Not my business. I gotta get you out of here, though. Keep a hand on my shoulder. Use my body as your shield."

"Don't think I won't."

Hal stopped. "You really messed with my head in Turkey."

"Would it help if I said, when I'm done with this, I'll come home and let you kick my ass?"

Hal gave a single, quiet laugh. "What would be new about that? I've always kicked your ass."

They moved down a day-over/dark, business office corridor. Slowly, carefully out the back. Hal saw his target half a second before he saw Hal and Michael; because the man was there to abduct Michael, he was fatally slow. Two silenced rounds, center mass, at distance. Michael watched his brother go to the body, turn the man's head with his toe and take a photo with his mobile phone. Put a third round in his forehead to be certain. Took his handgun. A bulky Glock.

"No silencer. Thug gun. Coercion effect. Want it?"

Michael took it. Hal nodded at the dead man's vehicle. "Come on. You got somewhere you can go?"

Michael sniffed the barrel. "Put to use for more than coercion—" Ejected the magazine. Checked the bullets with pressure from his thumb. "Two times."

Hal caught the dread creeping into his brother's face. "No. No way. You can't go back there."

Michael charged the car. Jumped behind the wheel. "Get in."

♔ ♔ ♔

RANSACKED, though not robbed, the Laundernet was in ruins. Likewise, Helene Favre's apartment upstairs. Vicious and vindictive. Whoever had done this had been searching only for her; denied the taking of her life, they transferred their aggression to the destruction of that life's possessions and mementos, decorations and memorials. Michael drew some relief that she'd had the good sense to get while the getting was good, but with an equal sense of self-recrimination. Had she not chosen to remove herself, he'd not suggested it to her. He needed to be certain she was safe. Hal covered the top of the stairs with his weapon. After a few minutes' search, Michael found a photo of Helene and her husband. Geneva Harbor. The *Échalote*.

"There are a dozen probabilities and outcomes that make this a bad idea. For you and for her."

"Look, we'll leave the car. We'll make a clean approach. Surveil—make sure we're not walking into an ambush. But that woman needs to be warned. Needs to be protected."

"If she's dead?"

Michael's face—hunted, lonely eyes baleful. Their focus turned inside. He could not find words to express himself, or map what future would lie beyond if Hal's words turned out to be prophetic. He mumbled, "Don't come if you're chickenshit."

Hal shook his head. Clapped Michael on the shoulder—hand lingering briefly in solidarity—and walked past him to take the lead.

4.

I N 1972, BRIGHT-EYED AND rosy-cheeked, Nancy Wilmont walked into the Central Intelligence Agency with a degree in statistics from Cal Poly San Luis Obispo and took a shared cubicle and swivel chair in a classified only-because-it-was-Langley division of pay-roll. Lynn didn't know whether it had been Rusty Aiken and their wild sexcapades during Nancy's engagement to another man—Lynn never wanted to know about that in the first place—or Nathan Muir who had gambled with the young woman's life in an off-the-books operation with Aiken and Bishop out of the U.N. in 1976, but one of them or the other, or both in tandem, had identified a genius/poise/curiosity inside this young woman that, weighed with their own guilt at having mistreated/mis-used her, not only saw to her continued promotions, but encouraged her into every possible paid-sabbatical study program available. By the time Nancy Wilmont retired early from the CIA in 2005, she had amassed US government bought and paid masters and undergradu-ate degrees and technical certificates in digital foren-sic accounting, electronic data science, international law, computer systems research, simulation/model de-velopment and prototyping, software design. With each degree, each promotion, her security clearance, her power, and her mad-mathematical computational investigative skills grew and grew. Sadly, so did Nancy. She amassed mass. Her retirement—which wouldn't fly today—was a forced medical disability due to extreme obesity.

I lay it at your feet, Rusty. You used her and abused her and left a hole in her heart that she filled with Yum-Yum Donuts. (How's that for projection? Miss Tanqueray fill-in-the-year or the coffee mug.) He did call her Numbskull Nancy to her face—that was not okay...even if it made Nancy laugh.

Lynn hadn't called ahead. Couldn't have if she'd wanted to, and she hadn't wanted to because she couldn't afford to get a "no" answer. Now, facing one another across Nancy Wilmont's La Plata, Maryland, doorstep, Lynn and the former CIA whizbang accountant wore the expressions one sees on playgrounds when two kids—still relatively new to running—accidentally plow full-tilt into each other.

"What happened to you?!" *Jinx*—as Nancy spoke Lynn's thoughts.

It was obvious with Lynn, a week out from a homicidal cut-throat injury. She should be in a hospital bed. But Nancy?

If she turns sideways, I won't be able to see her.

Lynn typed: *Me—work accident. But you look amazing.*

Lynn forced a smile, which only caused Nancy deeper confusion, lofted, as it was, over a throat bandage and a P/M valve. Nancy said, "This is what nineteen grand with no one to spend it on and a SADI procedure can do for a tubby girl." She stepped aside. "Come-come, Lynn." The living room. "Sit-sit. Has Rusty popped back into our lives and gotten himself in trouble?"

Lynn typed: *No. Thank goodness.*

"Well, that's good. Minus two hundred pounds, I probably wouldn't be able to keep my hands off him again. Oh, did I do a number on him."

Lynn typed: *I thought it was sort of the other way around.*

Nancy guffawed. "Everyone did! Including my ex-husband, including Nathan—I'll tell you—did you know I was Miss Camarillo 1969? Out in California? You'd think the beauty pageant code would be a lot of females all looking out for each other, but the men, who weren't gay, I was in trouble with since I was way too young, and college—I was lucky I was born smart, let's just put it that way—but for me, I was practically born with the sex drive of a seventeen-year-old boy, and after college it was either the nunnery or the CIA. They—the Agency—came on so cold and dull and serious and sexless, I thought I'd be safe from myself. Oh, Rusty—" She sighed, then gave Lynn a penetrating look. "He'd like *this.*"

Lynn gaped. Already exhausted. Typed: *You don't say.*

Nancy got it. Laughed again. "I'm sorry. No one visits me. I don't go to church anymore, because I'm shunned as home-wrecker danger—and they're probably right; I got the gals at the grocery store, used to have the post office, but who sends letters anymore? And, gosh, I'm doing it again, and—Wow! One of Nathan's orchids. Look at you—you can't tell me anything about it, I'm sure, but you must be doing a little independent/extracurricular to come here—"

Lynn interrupted, flipping her tablet for Nancy to see. *This is off the edge of acceptable/legal. I'm here to ask you to break vows stricter than a nun's.*

Nancy stilled."You wouldn't be here, and I wouldn't have let you in if I didn't understand the difference between what vows can be broken and those that can't." Dead serious.

Lynn typed: *What's a Nathan orchid?*

"Nathan Muir had about ten officers, including Rusty, Danny Aiken, Tom Bishop, Lara van Eyck, that tragic Amy Kim—and Nina—what a star we had in Havana—and of course you, that Nathan designated as his ORCHIDS. He never told me, but I suspect because all of you are/were rare, and precious and needed extra-special care in order to bloom spectacularly."

Lynn: *There were others?*

Nancy sidestepped back to the playground and did the finger-zipper across her lips. But that lasted all of one second, and she said, "Tell me what you've got, and I will see what I can do."

Lynn typed: *It's hardware/software technical.*

Nancy walked to the accordion dining-room door and slid it open. "Don't use the room for eating anymore."

Fans whirred, drives hummed, screens flickered. Lynn offered Nancy her burner phone.

"I can get in, and I can get a one-time look. But once I get past the encryption, we're going to be in a digital footrace. To open the architecture around these files requires it to think it is communicating with its original server. I can make it think that. But soon after I do, maybe thirty seconds—one minute on the outside—it will seek security reauthentication. Like asking for a token to keep the meter running. I won't be able to provide it and it will digitally corrupt and delete. Judging from the size—" she did an odd thing with her hands; she smoothed them down the sides of her narrow ribcage. "That will take about one minute."

Lynn typed: *That's not good.*

"But not impossible. Once I'm in, my program snapshots every page. But because the security protocol deletes data randomly, it's like whack-a-mole trying to get any actual whole or even readable pages before it's all gone."

Lynn tapped out: *I can't believe I'm writing this, but it's kind of exciting.*

"I live for excitement. Ready?"

Lynn nodded.

One minute and twenty seconds later, Nancy printed out eighteen non-sequential pages of account ledgers.

She peered over the edge of the papers, over the edge of her half-lens reading glasses. "Good news is I know exactly what I'm looking at—which is also the bad news."

Lynn typed: *You've encountered these accounts before?*

"No, no, not these specifically. No. Thank God. But back in the eighties, the Banco Ambrosiano flap—Vatican/mafia/CIA money laundering—I received my first big security bump. I was part of the accounting team that dug in to assess our exposure and vulnerability."

Lynn: *Iran-Contra?*

"The Contras, yes, and the Polish Solidarity movement; admittedly, we were trying to cover what tracks we could. Ten years later, the same accounting practices—meaning Agency fingerprints—came up in the BCCI scandal."

Lynn: *Something to do with monitoring drug money laundering and arms dealers?*

"You don't make an omelet without breaking..."

Lynn mouthed, *Eggs?*

"You're running undercover, *participating* inside an illegal banking system for that number of years—eggs, legs, necks. Lots get broken when things go bad. My team was the kitchen towel. And what we discovered and got our operations out of were several other dark banks, dark accounts/transactions we shouldn't have been involved with, spending money on things we shouldn't have been buying." She wagged the print-out pages. "These have the earmarks of being the big granddaddy of all of them. I see an entry here—and it's not millions, it's billions—that's 1973. This one alone just keeps growing."

Lynn typed: *That's unusual?*

"Extraordinarily. Typically—no, more than typically. Exclusively. These types of black accounts are created as spending accounts. You have your laundered money. Flows in. Flows out. There's a service fee collected on it. Plus, fast interest on massive sums. These go to pay your skim—there's always that. Plus, salaries—from the boardroom to the bank teller, courier. The rest is converted into black op financing. Weapons, secret bases, secret armies. It's money in constant movement. These—" she waved her pages. "Money comes in, but only small amounts, if anything ever goes out."

Lynn: *Savings accounts?*

"Appears that way." She switched to her last page. "And they're still amassing the wealth."

Lynn typed. *Public records show assets of close to two-and-a-half billion.*

"Everything else that isn't this. I'm looking at trillions. Plural. And here's the thing about savings accounts—you're always saving up for *something*."

Lynn's fingers danced. *What could need that kind of funding?*

"If you're bargain shopping—maybe a handful of nations? Maybe the infrastructure of one great big one?"

Lynn: *Lot's cheaper to start a color revolution, run an overthrow. Or, in the old days, flat-out assassinate the leader. Start a war—we've always been good at that.*

"And when was the time *any* of those got us anywhere good or anything permanent?"

Lynn typed/showed: *This is a CIA account. Confirm?*

"CIA patterned." A pointed look. "But the fact we never saw it, accidentally bumped against this Pell/Glatisant entity when we were set at cleaning this shit up, means the official—as in sanctioned by US Constitution—*we* of us, CIA? I doubt the Seventh Floor even knows about it."

Lynn: *I've compromised you?*

"You don't get fired or arrested for digging at this. You get killed." Nancy held out her hand. "Here, give me the SIM card. Untraceable, I hope?"

Out came the phone. Out came the SIM card. She watched Nancy snap it in two.

Sorry, Hal. You're on your own until you get back.

"These—" pages/SIM card pieces— "Hard drive, router, printer: they'll be burned and melted. Gone by tonight. My IP address is untraceable. I'll be just fine." A steady look. "We just crept up and took a peek from behind at a sleeping dragon. Do not poke him, do not touch him, blow in his ear—whatever you're after, find another angle. Tiptoe away from this as far away as you can. The only worse enemy than the enemy is us."

♛ ♛ ♛

LYNN SAT ON the wooden bench in front of the Centennial Street US Post Office in La Plata, where Janella would pick her up in about thirty minutes. Slid her tablet—pre-typed—to Morton Drexler as he sat beside her.

He picked it up. Read: *Why didn't you follow me when I walked?*

"I'm not stupid. As you always prove yourself to be. If you hang, she'll hang too—I can make a rope strong enough."

Lynn typed: *Happy to report she's not gargantuan like you anymore. You obviously don't want to make this official—so what is it you want?*

"Save you from yourself when it goes official. Whatever you, Michael, and your GI Joe brother are mixed up in, aims back at your father. You can either ride above it in the airplane or be on the ground when the bomb hits. I'm blowing up, Silas Kingston."

Lynn: *Not so nice a way to treat your second daddy.*

Drexler stood. Hitched his pants. "Get that voice healed. If it comes down to it, it'll make interrogation/confession that much easier."

5.

THE ROOM 224 AIR conditioner against the window—Super 8/Route 235/Lexington Park, MD—did nothing to cut the heat boiling between Clive Lancer and his control, Fergus Jones.

"Switch from transmit to receive and read me: I'm not doing it. Over—like my part of this whole fucking op!"

"You don't get to make that call!"

"You don't get to tell me where I put my dick! She's an innocent girl!"

"The magic moonlight. The stroke of midnight. Womanhood bestowed." Mocking laugh. "What happened to my Randy-Andy? Couldn't get Little Willy to open his eye?"

Clive threw a fist that, expecting it, Fergus caught. Twisted Clive's arm behind his back. Jacked it up. Threw him onto the bed. Towered over him. Fists clenched.

"You don't want to go there, laddie."

Clive glared. Didn't otherwise move.

"You may be proud, you may be moral, you may think you two have matching hearts, and you're her white knight with a pink plume coming out your arse, but we are keeping you in there; you are going to compromise a Kingston, and once we have a little leverage, you're going to tear that place down—get that stupid cow to do whatever I want—until between the two of you, you find us something we can use against the old shitter to bring him justice."

"*A* Kingston?"

Fergus keyed up some photos on his phone.

"You've been fucking surveilling me?!"

"Doing my job. This one's not only going to spread 'em for you. She's going to wrap those legs around you like an anaconda around a baby pig. *Oink-oink.*"

"You're sick. That's a thousand ways worse."

With a sound like pebbles, rain pattered the fogged/humid window above the air conditioning unit. Fergus's contempt for the younger man blazed in his eyes.

"Back across the ocean, where the flag you answer to flies, they consider it my best idea yet. The mum already hates her father-in-law. She's conflicted over her husband. A CIA officer in his own right."

"I am aware of that. Michael Kingston's current situation has nothing to do with our investigation of his father and his boogeyman past."

Fergus bridled at the flippancy.

"It's called leverage, you twat. To get it, she just needs a little push and a squeeze." Fergus sat on the bed. "Come on. You'd throw away your career and your freedom? But you're in luck. You're cleared to receive an incentive."

Clive backed up against the headboard. A sullen, "What incentive?"

"Silas Kingston. That most promising young CIA officer, kicking around Moscow in 1971 with his even younger wife—a lass not much older than your sweet, innocent Paige. Her guidschir-and-lord up and does something a wee bit wobbly. Offended us greatly. Offended our Queen, so greatly, she has never forgotten. It is not something our service will ever forgive. A fairy tale with a monster to kill at the end."

Thunder rolled like ancient army drums.

"Spooky," Clive taunted.

"Shut your mouth and listen."

❦❦❦

AS THOUGH AN ORCHESTRAL roll of timpani, thunder drummed Paige into her birthday. Relatively early—phone read: 9:20—her mom and the girls already up; from where she lay on a porch sofa, she could hear everyone clattering/chattering/laughing about in the kitchen. Her head felt—surprisingly—pretty good.

You cried out all the alcohol.

Her pillow—still damp. Yet she didn't feel the least bit sad. Not anymore.

Not a bit. I'm eighteen. What was that Latin word from class?

Dictum—a noun derivative from the neuter of dictus, past participle of dīcere: "to talk, speak, say, utter." Dictum. A formal proposition.

Dictum: I am officially an American adult. I can leave my home and my family. I can get a job if I want, without permission; I can get an apartment, take my classes at a college I want—knock out my general ed requirements; I can take a gap year and divert my life on a path of my own choosing. I can go get my driver's license without permission. I can buy a rifle. Join the army! I don't need to have sex with some dude just to prove it.

She stared at the rain, and, though it was hard and obscuring, the spectrum of light that passed through the gray clouds radiated green; vividly enhancing the lawn, the trees, the moss bearding the wet, gray chapel walls, the overgrown near fields—all of it so vibrant, a silent shout of life without the wash-out glare of the sun. The falling rain obscured but this vigorous green hooked in Paige's stomach. Spoke to her gut. Balance, vitality, serenity. Green.

A weight had been bearing down on Paige. Just last week, pushing her from her family/her childhood with a kind of need that she must prove herself to her future, hew her from her past. She was hewn to both her past and her future by her present. *That* was most important. She was not on the edge of anything. Would never have to be if she lived for the center of her own and personal "now."

I shouldn't have sulked so much on the drive home. Clive felt horrible—noticeably; I was embarrassed, and I shouldn't have been. God, why do you always let me act like such an idiot? I didn't even let him kiss me goodnight when he dropped me off.

He'll either be here today or he won't. If he is, all I can do is be real.

She watched the rain roll up from the river and over the manor. A series of racing squalls.

Deeb. What an asshole. But I contributed to it. Let both of us get wasted. Teased him and pushed him—I wanted to get laid. For all the wrong reasons. He shouldn't have done what he did, but I was playing with fire. Screwing at the beach bonfire wasn't going to make me a woman; last night wasn't going to do that either. I tried to use both of them: one was a full-on m-f'er and the other was a man about it. An old-fashioned gentleman.

Sex—losing my virginity. That doesn't make me a woman.

Eighteen hasn't made me a woman.

I am a woman.

Charlotte poked her head through the French doors. "Paige! It's your birthday! Get up and come have breakfast!"

Leigh's head popped out beside her. "Start celebrating, lazybones! Wooo!"

"Give me a minute, you guys. C'mon. I will."

I am going to celebrate. Show everyone I love—who loves me—who I am by what they mean to me.

Paige jumped on her phone. Instagram. New Post. Dug deep in her album. Found/attached six pics. Caption: *Best Sisters Ever!* Hashtagged Charlotte. Hashtagged Leigh. Ten minutes more coming up with every "sister-y" tag she could think of. Aimed her finger at "Post," hesitated—

School.

#Pancrashallclassof2016

#Pancrashallclassof2020

Again, about to hit Post, she noticed her grandfather. Closing/locking the North Vista door. Through the rain, through the window, Silas noticed Paige. She hit the button as she dashed outside to meet him, hearing the *ding...ding* from the kitchen as the screen screeked closed behind her.

"Happy birthday, Paige."

"Quick! I need to borrow your car."

Ever unflappable. "Where we going?" Silas tossed keys.

They caught the sun. A flash of orange dappled through the tenebrous boughs of the pines, Paige caught the keys, and her birthday spun into a kaleidoscopic blur: The Cadillac. Chased by sisters waving phones. Faces like what's going on? The "Likes" chiming in—Paige's phone loud, their *dings* stalling them to stop, look, wonder, and out the gate. Into town. We won't find much that's open and Paige said the drugstore's always open, to which Silas asked if something happened the night before. Paige laughed in his face—I'm not going there for *that*. Good; the place for burying boyfriends on the property is already full-up.

A roll of her eyes. A wide turn into the lot—the stick on the steering wheel works your blinker, kiddo—and into the store. Over to the kids' pool/beach/toy aisle. To the small jewelry case. The guy—let me get my key. To the gift card rack. Back to the kids' aisle. Two packs of the nifty-new 100 water balloons fill all at once like her heart with the euphoria filling inside of it. A false start to the cashier. Back to the gift cards. A switcheroo. And her phone, *ding, ding, dinging* with Instagram "Likes."

Back to Foxtail Farm. The Cadillac on the highway, glowing yellow as the sunlight heated and dried the air. Beneath the pine, in through the gate, back to the east porch—

"Happy Birthday, Paige!" "Where'd you go?" "I can't believe you'd embarrass me to *everyone!*" "What's in the bags?" "I didn't know you had a picture of me from when I learned to dive off the rock." "You know I have four open houses to do *before* your birthday. I wanted to give you a hug/go-and-come-back—What time are your friends coming?" Jack, Leigh, Charlotte, Little Silas, Leigh (again). Gwen. Walking past—Paige: Where's Aunt Melody? In here, babe. And simultaneously, dogging Paige's steps, Little Silas, grabbing at the big plastic shopping bag— "Did you get toys? Are those toys? Did you get toys or something fun?" *Ding. Ding. Ding.*

Into the kitchen, Paige flung eyes over her shoulder. "Girls, those 'likes' aren't for me." Charlotte/Leigh: thumbs bouncing on screens. "Hooo-ly kamoley!"/giggly-squeal. Out of the bag: sandcastle molds: blue and yellow set, red and green set; water balloons, two packs flung over her shoulder—general direction of her sisters. A little bag from inside the big bag. To Melody. "I was going to get you a massage card." Gwen, fluffing black curls in the mirror, lipstick touch-up, kiss-kiss reflection, "I hope you got one for your mom!" Dragonfly hover—still there/not left—and Paige remembered how Melody really wanted a medium saucepan. Gwen laughs. At Paige. At Melody. Didn't matter; Melody couldn't believe Paige knew she even wanted a saucepan at all, and yes, Bed, Bath and Beyond would be a perfect place to get it—how-did-you-even-know?

Direct look: "I listened at some point, I guess."

Better have got that massage card for me. Gwen. Second little bag. From the big bag. Wrapped in tissue. Not a card. Silver-plated chain/silver-plated cross. Gwen's oh and Silas saying the appropriate thing is to put it on, and Gwen I *am* putting it on. Paige: Sort of matches mine—

"The one I got that was Grandma Doris's." Gwen offered the ends of the chain. Offered the back of her neck.

Paige offered this: "It's kind of for you *and* Dad."

And Leigh with an Ah! You made Mom get fat lip. True to form. Gwen's lower lip did jut and her dark eyes went misty. A thank you, hun, a kiss, a check the Cartier, and the kiss-off dragonfly side-sweep out the door gone.

Everyone in bathing suits. Everyone outside. Everything sparkly after the rain. Prism rainbows rising from the lawn: one hundred thousand silver-edged scissor blades in the pure white sunshine of summer. The water balloon fight, fast, fun. Harmless brutal excitement. Interrupted once: Charlotte and Leigh—Time out! Times! Time out! —checking a new flurry of *dings*. Interrupted twice: Morgan arrived, Clive minutes behind, and Paige hugged, kissed them both the same way—best friends—because that's where it started with Morgan, that's where she needed it to go back, to begin again with Clive. Paige's teeth gleamed and ready to get drenched? Clive relaxed. Opened. Filled the second bag of water balloons. The second battle joined fun/brutal/soaking wet until Little Silas and Jack bored/anxious/excited to build castles dragged Clive prisoner to the beach stairs.

Time stopped. Melody hugged Paige. "You are a beautiful eighteen, Paige. And you know what?"

"What?"

"I love you."

Should have been her mom; should have cared about that but didn't. The moment belonged to itself. Paige grabbed her aunt's hand, pulled her for the stairs. About to prance down—from behind— "Happy birthday, Paige!" Hands released, Paige and Melody whip around, hair tumbly, in synch and like they planned it for a dance, with Janella finishing from Lynn's tablet, "Who gives out gifts on their birthday?"

Lynn. On the porch steps. Leaning too much on the handrail. Pale with exhaustion. Needed a bed. Needed back in the hospital. Paige: "I'm still getting yours!" Lynn pressed her hand to her heart. Blew it, her heart imaginary, off her palm. She and her nurse turned back inside; Paige and her aunt turned for the beach and descended out of sight.

No one left but Silas. On the North Vista porch. Hadn't moved since Paige parked and left him with his keys.

He judged it all.

Felt gifted allowed to witness Paige's elation, the elasticity of time made to exhilarate; were he removed from this life dead/alive, this family he'd given everything for—right/wrong, good/evil, heaven pled and hell delivered—Paige could bring together in pieces to a center-place picture of family in reality.

👑👑👑

THERE WAS THE BEACH. There was the BBQ—I'm not as good at this as Uncle Hal—and the truth that Melody was better. So easily. Lynn rested outside as afternoon cooled into her own private, everything-about-to-be-sunsetted evening. But not yet, so Lynn is shrugging worry and loving on her niece and projecting future alternatives for Leigh.

Where will we be?

How will we love?

What will we know?

Carefully and under care, Lynn ate Melody's Carolina chopped pork. Ate molasses baked beans, and the twins stared—and Leigh and Charlotte, too, but hid it better. Paige scooted close on the picnic bench.

Direct: "Remember when you'd send me running up and down the beach to find these when I was little?" She gave Lynn her gift. "I've never seen a piece this color of Grandma Doris's dress before."

♛ ♛ ♛

PAIGE AND CLIVE swim around the mermaids. Take turns on how far down they can go. Clive bubbles up. "There're words written on these."

"Shut up."

"Seriously. Charlotte, throw us your goggles!"

Goggles thrown. Lost. Found. Thrown again and lost and found again and swum out and handed over.

All three of them tread water together.

"It's your birthday." Clive helps the googles over Paige's head. Slender legs to the sky. Dolphin kick down. Water parts across her rising face. With a gasp— "'The Lord giveth.' On the first one."

"'And the Lord taketh away—'I betcha. Let me look!" Charlotte.

But Paige glides down again. Too much black algae on the second cypress post to tell. Rubs and scratches. Kicks back to surface. Breathless. Clings to the post. "Give me that beach glass I put in your Velcro pocket. It's all mossy. Maybe I can scrape it."

Clive hands it over. Paige submerges... Bursts forth in diamond droplets.

"It says, 'The water showeth forth.' Is that from the Bible?"

Charlotte snatches her goggles from Paige's face. Sinks feet first to see for herself.

Clive contemplates Paige. She is the mermaid. She is the siren. She is the shoal he yearns to dash his life and career, his fortunes against. Paige sees his sadness. Sees his longing. His verge of revelation.

Charlotte sputters. "You guys! That's not *what it says. I rubbed it more. The second post. The E-T-H are scratched out. Something is scratched next to them."*

"All right, all right. Clive's turn," he says. Grabs the goggles.

The three letters are X'd out. Beside the T and the H—carved later and with less depth and less precision—are a U and an S. He floats. He stares. The kaleidoscope slows and stops.

The Lord giveth

The water show us forth.

6.

L YNN'S FACE, RARELY SOFT, radiated warmth and admiration. She leaned forward. Whispered, croaked, and dry, "Never had one this red before."

Cake and candles. The song. There were presents. There was nightfall. With it, scent of earth and grass and pine sap as if the private world of the Kingstons, having held its breath through the heat of that golden July day, sighed a collective breath, and people and the creatures, the birds and the insects all chilled into the secret business of darkness.

The Reverand Vivianne Tremelin had joined them for dinner. Blessed the meal, and when she blessed Paige, Morgan and Clive met eyes across the table with looks that seemed to remark how quaint and isn't it special, a thing like that—they didn't believe themselves—could be so magical for Paige?

There was magic in Gwen's eyes—devilish—every time she caught Clive eying her.

The gifts were mostly clothing (though Clive gave her fancy earbuds, which Paige liked most of all), and the girls—the twins too, because their cousins were cheering for it—begged a fashion show. Paige wanted to wait for Silas's present, but he had gone to walk Vivi to her car. It was getting late for the twins. No need to wait.

Melody told Paige to use the exercise room on the west porch. It was good for its lighting, good for its floor-to-ceiling mirrors. Charlotte and Leigh helped Paige carry her boxes inside. They crossed through the interior of the house, straight from one porch to the other.

"Okay. I'll be out in a minute."

Alone. Thinking of Clive.

We can start over. We are already. We make a good match.

Felt warm. Felt safe. She basked in that moment until her eyes lit upon a time-worn, yellowed box she had never seen before. She lifted the lid. Paige opened the folds of tissue paper. Time and place lost themselves to infinity/eternity as Paige beheld the dress. Her heart hammered. Was this Papa's gift? Was it a test?

But Papa was already gone when Melody said I should come change out here in back.

Red sequins dazzled the light. Paige gingerly lifted Doris's dress from its box.

♕ ♕ ♕

LEIGH ASKED Melody: "I've been memorizing the Paul Revere poem. Do you want to hear how far I've gotten?"

She did, and they were doing the *Midnight Ride*, and Morgan was occupied doing magic tricks with a coin. A simple magic where you make a penny disappear from one hand and pull it out of a kid's ear/nose/mouth with the other—and Jack and Little Silas were busting up and enthralled. They didn't believe it—

"It isn't real! It's not possible!"

"Who says I'm not a witch?"

They wanted to learn it. They checked their own ears when they thought no one else was looking.

Clive slipped off.

Gwen slipped off.

PAIGE SLIPPED OFF her beach cover-up. Slipped off her bathing suit. A silk slip also from the box. She pulled it over her head; it shimmered as she shimmied into it.

MELODY'S PHONE buzzed. She checked it. Held her reaction in check. The same text she'd received two nights back from Arkansas.

"Coming soon, child. 4u & 4 them. Better have found it."

"YOU SURE THIS IS OKAY with you?" Gwen to Clive, already in his arms.

"Is this okay with you?" Paige asked the air. The house. Asked Doris, and as soon as she had, it felt less wrong than right. She took the pink Nikes given her by her sisters. Laced them on. She turned out the lights. Suddenly nervous about letting Doris see her in the interior mirrors. Paige went the long way. Made the turn from the west porch onto the southern facing side.

When lights are on inside a house, window glass becomes opaque. Reflective. When lights are off, and especially when there is a good moon, as there is tonight, the glass is a lens to all beyond. Shapes stand out from shadows. The mind sorts them into pictures.

Through the south porch windows, between trees, and across a short corner of field, Paige saw the ramshackle ruins of an ancient tobacco drying shed. The one without a roof. The one with gaps in its weathered plank walls. Inside one of the gaps, two figures in a frame. Her mother pressed Clive's hands to her breasts beneath her shirt; he pressed his body to hers, their faces locked in passion.

Scream, cry, laugh, rage, ice cold wave up spine and into brain, and storm and whimper; the urge to howl and the inability to breathe. Why am I smiling/stupid? Why does it hurt and my tears won't stay behind my eyes?

Fuckers.

She was running between the trees when the screen door smacked like the shot of a pistol. Sequins summoned the moon; scintillated on vibratory waves of stirring fabric.

A wave of supernatural fear hit Gwen. Her flesh crawled. Up her arms, the rising hair. Doris rushed her straight from hell. Flew directly into her.

Paige put all she had behind her shoulder. Checked her mother as hard as she could, toppling her into the weeds, the high grass and bramble. Gwen let the wine do the talking. She laughed and said, "He's a grown man! What did you expect?!"

Legend has it that Turkey John Swann hanged runaways in that drying shed. In a moonlit-warped-time way, Clive almost appeared noosed-up. Proud and defiant. Appalled by his guilt. Willing to step from an imagined tobacco bundle and take the air, never to feel solid ground again.

Paige stopped hard. "You're so fucking transparent. I was right. You're still working this family."

He looked directly out from his soul into her heart. "I'm absolutely gutted. Nothing I can say can express how sorry I am."

"I don't care."

Rage gone. Tears gone. Heart: gone. Walk away.

He spoke to her back. "Men sometimes have to sacrifice to make hard decisions for a greater cause."

Paige turned. "When you become a man—one without a pull-string—you'll understand exactly how true that statement is and how hardcore you failed it tonight."

He yelled after her. "Your grandfather gave up seven of our Russian agents! They were executed! Their handlers—three British officers—murdered! People like me!"

She stopped. "I don't believe it. I don't believe screwing my mom will get you the answer to it, either. But dance on your puppet string all you want. I won't blow your sick-fucking cover, and, more than I thought I could love you? I want to see you miserable. I want to see you fail."

Don't take eyes off him. He knows I'm right. It's gonna drive him crazy because he doesn't know what to do, and I can't believe I said all that.

Her stomach lurched.

Run. Before you lose it. Run!

MELODY, AND LYNN, Morgan—they'd seen Gwen stumble from the overgrown field; they heard her sobs as she slammed into the house. Clive was nowhere to be seen, and they could guess what that meant. Paige ran out—the living ghost of Doris flashing red—and Melody couldn't quite conceal her horror. Covered her mouth to squelch her cry.

Paige ignored them all. Slammed inside the chapel.

Melody lurched to follow, but Lynn grabbed her wrist. "I thought—Where'd she get—"

Lynn hissed, "You can't help her with this."

Morgan covered the grin on her face. Didn't want the others to see that side of her. In truth, she really had something witch-like about her; and Clive? He must have climbed the neighbor's wall, fled through the orange orchard, because he never reappeared that night, which Lynn and Melody later agreed was the best thing for him to have done.

♔ ♔ ♔

SMOKE. Burned wax. Fresh lilies. Old wood. Old stone, old books, old silver and gold and brass, and stained glass. Old and handstitched, pressed linen. Stone and metal polish and oiled wood. Candlelight bounced and flickered and reflected/refracted/rebounded. A head-swirling assault on Paige's senses; she staggered to the marble-seamed edge of Doris's tomb.

The execution of seven of our Russian agents! The murder of three British officers! Their handlers! People like me!

Tears stained her cheeks, but she cried without a sound. Broad hands seized her from behind.

Silas turned Paige into his arms. Crushed her tightly to his chest. Let her cry, but only a moment or two before he held her out at arm's length. "Do you need me to tell you why he did that?" The dress did not surprise him.

"Because Mom's a slut and a bitch?"

An accepting smile. "Because your mother is childish and has always had a screw loose since Michael first brought her home. What she's done is unconscionable. Do you know why he let her?"

Her eyes went dry. Focused on his face.

He knows...

"Do you, Paige?"

She wouldn't answer.

"Good for you, then." Silas added. "You know what I've always said about this place? Foxtail Farm?"

"You don't stick your hand into a fox's den."

"Let me look at this dress."

Paige struck a soft and noble pose. Hardly felt brave, but was. "It's too much of a present."

"I'll be the judge of that."

"I told him I wouldn't blow his cover. I feel so stupid."

"You may not believe me, but I'm proud of you for that."

Silas took her hand. He led her to the altar. They kneeled. He said, "As for the rest? Let that be between he and I."

"Him and I."

He kissed her brow, then crossed himself.

Paige crossed herself.

Silas: "If he is half the man that we both know he has inside himself, he won't put you in the middle of settling it."

Elbows on the rail, they each folded their hands together. Both prayed. Their secrets and their dreams. Prayed for protection from their sins. For a little while, they found sanctuary inside the family church.

♚ ♚ ♚

No ambush at the dock. Hal boarded the *Échalote* first, Michael pressing hard behind him. No sign of a struggle. The cabin door stood ajar. Hal pressed Michael hard against the bulkhead. Forced him to wait. He went through the door, almost eager to exchange fire. "Clear!"

The main cabin. "Clear! Clear!" The two berths. He looked back for Michael. His brother was gone.

Helene lay supine on the black-painted foredeck. Starlight winked from behind billowing curtains of enveloping fog that spread toward the harbor from the distant center of the lake. Michael crouched beside Helene. He clutched her hand. Stared at the blood seeping through her trim, down shell. Burned nylon edges around a mess of wet-red feather stuffing. Her heart beat no more.

"Nothing we can do here, Michael." A hand on his shoulder. "I'm sorry, but we gotta go. Right now."

"No." Michael shook off Hal's hand. Turned his face. Loss. Confusion. Desperation. "It shouldn't a'been mom in her picture."

"What? What picture? This woman had a picture of our mother?"

"If anyone—it should have been Dad."

"C'mon." Hal reached out again.

Michael batted his hand.

"Get a grip, bro." And Hal grabbed him. "We're going." Pulled him hard. "Now."

Michael wrenched free. Threw Hal against the pilot-house windows. "I'm not going anywhere."

"It hurts. It's bad. Assets get killed—" He gathered— "Now grow a pair and move it." Seized him. Michael struggled. "Michael: do not do this to me again. We're fucking going!"

Michael wedged both hands hard against Hal's chest. Shoved him onto the port side deck. "She wasn't a fucking asset."

"She died as one." Hal baited—took another shove—backing them both toward the stern.

"She was innocent! I used up her life!"

"Nature of our business, bro." Hal drew another shove, tripping backward, angling them for the gangway ramp.

"Haven't you fucking figured it out yet?!" Shove. "She wasn't our business." Shove. Madness in his eyes. "This is what our family does!" Shove. Spit flying— "We destroy everyone we touch!"

Michael shoves air—Hal ducking in, getting him around the waist, bouncing Michael into the gangway stanchion.

"You're coming with me." Hal spun him. Snarled in his ear. "While you're dicking around chasing 'poor me,' mama's boy ghosts—" aimed him for the dock— "and getting innocent people— yeah, you're fucking right about that—killed, you're *losing* your family."

Michael set his feet. Braced. The brothers grappled at the top of the ramp.

"Gwen is trying to steal your girls from you! I've been forced to declare you dead! You're getting erased—erasing yourself—and I'm not getting trapped *here*, losing *my* wife and *my* kids—when you don't even fucking care what happens to yours!"

His fists flew. Michael took it. Blow for blow. With an animal cry, he threw Hal to the dock.

Michael hovered, menacing, wretched, body quaking as his soul pulled away from the present.

The Enchanted Forest. He sees his father weak and shrinking as the stranger kisses his mother's face. The man this boy admires most, physically shrinking, and he's staring at his son, weak, pathetic, and impotent.

Michael's hero.

His coward.

His shame.

Deranged, Michael cast lines. Pulled the ramp.

"You'll be arrested for murder."

Michael staggered into the cabin.

"And for stealing the boat!"

Hal remained on the dock as the engine engaged. "You can't get anywhere!" he shouted. "It's a fucking lake, you idiot!"

Michael headed into it. Into misty fingers that beckoned him enter the roiling fog.

In the strange twinkle of starlight through the fog, through the pilothouse window, Helene Favre's face came alive, not only as her own but as the faces of all the women Michael loved.

Came alive as Gwen.

Came alive as Doris.

Came alive as Lynn, as Paige, as Charlotte, and as Leigh. Michael broke down as they surrounded him. He slumped to the deck, tearing his hair and beating his head against the wheel housing. The seething fog engulfed the boat. Stole inside and enveloped Michael Kingston. Although his mind shrieked and whirled, Michael went still. His stare fixed blankly upon a crushed, damp piece of paper he had found protruding from Helene's mouth.

万花筒

He didn't understand Chinese. Didn't understand a thing. And the man he once had been was now well and truly lost.

ON TOP OF THE WIDOW'S WALK on the North Vista Out-house, Silas waited. The owl didn't call. The carrion crow weathervane with the bone in its beak was still. Silas had been sympathetic to Melody's surprised reaction to the Doris dress—although this would turn out to be for the wrong reason entirely. He'd not meant to frighten her. He'd meant for the dress to draw reaction from Lynn who played with fire she thought that she and her brothers—careers/lives/souls—were proofed against; he chose the dress for Paige to demonstrate that the fire you don't expect can either be the one that consumes you, or puts the others, unexpected, into clearer distinction, easy light when flashed—as always fires will—to flame.

He didn't wait long before Lynn let herself out the front door. *Beeped* her way into her car. Threw gravel out the gate, launched into the night on the Porsche's power of 390 horses. Satisfied that Lynn was taking the burden of her fate and future with her, Silas went downstairs. He placed a call from the encrypted phone, long ago installed, almost never used.

It rang a desk telephone inside an office on Constitution Avenue within the massive stone walls of the Herbert C. Hoover Building. Inside the Office of Treaty Regulation and Administrative Compliance. An office implemented after the signing of the Hay-Bunau-Varilla Treaty of 1903, which saw the United States recognize the nation of Panama after their breakaway from Columbia. OTRAC became the central collection point and legal library for US international treaties, "old world" nineteenth and twentieth century accords that ran smoothly out their course. Over its century-plus existence, OTRAC had been variously mocked as the Office Where Treaties Went to Pasture, as the Office of Obsolete Paper, until somewhere in the 1960s it was forgotten.

Less a branch than a twig of the Department of Commerce, OTRAC existed to sound the bulb horn if any international parlay or agreement negotiated by a current government crossed the paperwork detritus of its relics from governments past. The squeaker long removed, the horn no longer sounded, and, in that the Department of Commerce bore zero oversight from the Department of State, the Department of Defense, Department of Justice or any arm of the Intelligence Community writ large, small, or in invisible ink; in that its budget was a line item buried next to postage meter expenses in a digital communications age, it sat motionless, undisturbed and unencumbered.

OTRAC carried two full-time employees and an advisory board. Legal scholars and historians, on a don't-call-us, we'll-call-you honorarium gathered once a year for an all-expenses-paid Hay-Adams luncheon and a chance to ohh-and-aww at some documentary fossil dredged up for their after-meal entertainment. Director OTRAC—one of the two full-time employees—was an emeritus professor who took comfort in the extra salary the title conferred and would hold the position until their final breath, never knowing exactly what it was they'd directed. The Administrative Secretary was the only individual with a key to the office. The combinations to its safes. The encryption fob to its computers. And the authority to operate the telephone. Silas Kingston, if anyone had bothered to look, had been the last—1983-2010—AdSec OTRAC who, upon his retirement from the CIA, replaced himself with his many years Counterintelligence second-in-command.

"Double-checking that all went smoothly regarding my daughter?"

"Alas, alack, and good riddance."

"She's been removed." Silas repeated his original directive.

"Shuffled off as far far far—eh—from KALEIDO-SCOPE as you've required," said Meryl Hofmyer. "Welcome back, sir."

♛ ♛ ♛

A U Street Corridor three-level railroad house. The Duke Ellington historical area. Lynn's Porsche across the street and just outside the circle of a streetlamp. Between her legs, a bottle of gin. Seal yet uncracked. Her fists are clenched against her mouth. Knuckles block nostrils. She quivers and shakes. Stress/anguish/fury. She can block her natural airways indefinitely as her breath rasps through her tracheostomy tube.

After Paige runs past in her mother's dress—
After Melody—shaken more than she's ever seen—
After Silas nailed her with his most gloating smirk—

Lynn hears her cell phone chime inside the porch; Janella walks to her. Says, "It's Gary?" Lynn nods. "He says all you need to do is listen."

Lynn listens. Her world collapses. Morton Drexler? Her father? KALEIDOSCOPE?

Gary Gravin: "I warned you. You went too far, and there is nothing I can do to help. You will finish your medical leave. Heal—that's most important—but you won't be returning to Ops. This is from Harker's desk. As of your return, you will be assigned to Foreign Resources. As far from KALEIDOSCOPE and your brothers as possible. I'm sorry, Lynn, but I don't blame him. I'm glad it isn't worse."

Lynn stared at the house across the street. Three figures through the window. Jessie, Nina, Russell Aiken. Finish a card game. Jessie for all the tricks.

Lynn lowers one hand. Opens her fingers. Closes them over the screw-top lid. Twists.

Family hugs/kisses/goodnights. The women recede. Rusty steps to the window to draw the draperies. Something gives him pause. Looks to the pool of lamplight.

Lynn is outside the light. He cannot see her.

Lynn lifts the bottle with one hand. Opens the fist of her other.

Smooth red beach glass in her palm. Her mother's voice—

Broken glass cuts worst of all.

The smooth beach glass covers a wrinkled Polaroid snapshot, casting it the color of blood. Lynn stares at Russell Aiken with the longing of Eve at the closing Garden gate.

She's ours, Russell, that one impulsive time. She's ours.

♕ ♕ ♕

RUSSELL AIKEN reopened the draperies at the sound of burning rubber, the roar-off of an engine. A whiff of smoke hovered over a puddle. A bottle glugged onto the street. Gin spread across a Polaroid photograph of Lynn and Leigh Kingston. When Lynn was a mother; the day her child with Aiken was born.

Alcohol did its work and faded the image away.

About the author

AWARD-WINNING NOVELIST MICHAEL FROST Beckner began a Hollywood career as writing assistant to Academy Award winner Barry Levinson on "Good Morning, Vietnam" and "Rain Man". In 1989, Beckner's script for "Sniper" launched a military-thriller franchise now on its tenth sequel. Three consecutive record-breaking spec script sales and three films later, Tony Scott directed Beckner's original screenplay "Spy Game." An international hit that paired Robert Redford and Brad Pitt as CIA partners and rivals, it is now a classic in the espionage genre.

The pilot for Beckner's CIA-based television drama "The Agency" for CBS, predicted Osama bin Laden's terror attack and the War on Terror four months before 9/11. In that series alone, Beckner would go on to predict three more international terror events.

Having penned close to 100 original screenplays, adaptations, and teleplays in the employ of every major film studio, television network, and cable outlet, he is a Hollywood institution.

As a commentator on American espionage, Beckner has appeared on CNN, Fox News, CBS News, TF1 in France, and as a featured guest of Bill Maher on HBO.